To my wife, Pauline,
my children, Ben, Emily, Robert,
Alex, Oliver & Jack,
and my grandchildren,
Jasmine, Oscar & Matilda.

The Amazing Adventures of
Curd the Lion *and us!*
in the Land at the Back of Beyond

Alan Gilliland

Illustrated by
Alan Gilliland

Published in Great Britain by
Shabby Tattler Press, an imprint of
Raven's Quill Ltd.,
63, High Street, Billingshurst, West Sussex, RH14 9QP
01403-782489
www.ravensquill.com

British Library Cataloguing in Publication Data
A CIP record for this book can be obtained from the British Library.

ISBN 978-0-9555486-1-1

Printed and bound in China

Raven's Quill Ltd.,
63, High Street, Billingshurst, West Sussex, RH14 9QP
01403-782489
www.ravensquill.com

"I never had brother nor sister to incite such romps as make children familiar with nook and cranny," George MacDonald – Lilith

CONTENTS

BOOK I – The Amazing Adventures of Curd the Lion *and us!* In the Land at the Back of Beyond.

BOOK II *(a sampler)* – The Ineffable Emperor
or,
Travels to the Land of Nod in the Great Sea of Slumber, and of all that happened there.

WHERE WE WENT

PilgrimCrow

Labels on map: BRIMSTONE ROCKS, WRITING-DESK ROCK, CORBIE-STONE, DEAD TREE, CREVICE ROCK, FIRST-SIGHTING ROCK, BARN, STILE-GATE, HOLY WOOD, DAWLEY WOOD, OLD HAWTHORN TREE, MUMBIE'S HOUSE, BIRK-WOOD, MINE SHAFT, STILE, SIGN-POST, CLIFF, HAG'S BRIDGE, ZIGGUS MINES, MAGPIE MOOT, MILLPOND, HENRY'S HOUSE

CHAPTER ONE.   **St. George and the Dragon.**

"Up St. George!" yelled Henry.

Up flew Curd the Lion, leaving his tummy behind.

SWISH! Henry's sword whistled past Curd's ear.

Henry and Henrietta were playing St. George and the Dragon. Henry was St. George, Curd the yellow bean-bag Lion was the Dragon, and Henrietta was the Fair Damsel-in-Distress to be saved from the Dragon.

Down came Curd, landing on his tummy, THUMP!

"My Quest is done, Milady," shouted Henry. "I have slain yon Dragon and saved you, my Damsel-in-Distress!"

"Horray! Now it's my turn. I'm going to be St. George!" shouted Henrietta, louder, throwing off Mum's nightie that had been her cloak.

"And you can be the Damsel-in-Distress," she laughed.

"Of course I can't," said Henry, "I'm a boy. I can't be a Damsel-in-Distress."

"Then you can be the DamSon-in-Distress, then," cried Henrietta, "and I can be St. Georgette."

She grabbed his sword and helmet and shield and threw Mum's nightie over his head.

"Ugh!" groaned Henry, catching sight of himself in the mirror.

"No... Help! You've got to cry, Help!" said Henrietta. "Ok? Off we go!"

"Help!"

"I, the Questing knight, St.Georgette, will save you, fair Damson, from this beastly Dragon."

Up went Curd again, thinking that he had had enough of flying for today. "Die, Dragon, Die!" yelled Henrietta as she let fly with her sword.

WHACK! Henrietta's sword caught Curd in the middle of his thought and down he spun, clipping the dressing table.

CRASH! The talcum-powder jar and jewellery box tumbled to the floor with him, scattering Mum's jewellery all over the floor.

As a white cloud of talcum settled in every corner of the bedroom, Curd the Albino Lion lay staring up at the ghosts of Henrietta and Henry.

"Henry! Henrietta! What's all the racket about? What are you doing up there?" A shrill voice came up the stairs, followed closely by their mother.

The door to the bedroom opened and there stood the tall, slight, stooped figure of Mother staring down her long, beak-like, nose at them, her black hair a wild shock against the light on the landing behind.

"What on earth are you doing in my bedroom?" she screeched.

For a moment there was silence. Mother looked at Curd, lying frozen in the snowy waste that had been the bedroom carpet. She looked at Henrietta, the White Knight, waving her wooden sword in the air, foot planted firmly on Curd's back. She looked aghast. She didn't see Henry, who had disappeared into a little heap under her nightie.

"Look at the mess you've made, Henrietta!" Mum sat down on the bed and sprung back up again. "Henry! What are you doing in my bed – in my nightie, too? Get out, the pair of you. Go right outside immediately, with this hairbrush and Henry, brush Henrietta down until there's not a spot of white on her. NOW!"

The Twins ran straight downstairs, forgetting in their excitement to take Curd with them.

Curd the Lion was alone.

The winter winds howled viciously through the ghostly half-drawn lace curtains, rattling his thoughts like broken crockery. He could hardly hear himself think for shivering. Mother had opened the window wide to clear the air after clearing up the jewels and vacuuming up the talcum powder. She had accidentally kicked Curd so that he lay half under the bed, his nose and forepaws sticking out from under the candlewick counterpane's tickly tassles.

Slowly his thoughts began to glue themselves together. He reflected on the rough treatment meted out to Dragons. His ruminations (thoughts one thinks when all alone in a room) were rudely interrupted by a loud flapping noise and the startling appearance on the carpet in front of him of a deep black shadow that was neither that of the Twins nor their Mother.

He looked up to see the huge dark and sharply ragged shape of a monstrous winged creature standing on the window-sill. A DRAGON!?
Curd looked at the Dragon. The Dragon looked at Curd.

Curd was just wondering how to strike up a polite conversation with this distinctly unfriendly-looking Dragon, who didn't even say, "Hello," when the Dragon, without so much as a "May I come in and join you?" hopped down to join its shadow on the carpet.

The pair of them, black on black, strutted stiffly towards him.

The shadow smothered Curd with fright as the Dragon towered over him, cocking its swarthy long-beaked head first to one side, then to the other, its black beady eyes staring directly into Curd's shiny button-eyes. Summoning up all his courage, Curd opened up his mouth to roar.

Suddenly Curd realised this was no Dragon, but the Great Black Raven! He had heard the story about the Great Black Raven from their mother, who had told Henry and Henrietta how it came to fetch naughty children, and how it pecked out their eyes…

Perhaps it was the cold air from the open window, perhaps it was the prickling tightness of a cough coming on, but that terrifying ROAR seemed to stick somewhere deep in his throat.

Before he had time to work it out, the swarthy Raven leaned down over Curd and stabbed with its great black beak, snatching from right under his nose a glittering jewelled brooch. The sharp-eyed Raven must have seen it glinting in the winter sun through the open window. It was a brooch that Mother had accidentally kicked, together with Curd, under the edge of the bed as she cleaned the bedroom.

Curd was still speechless as the Raven flapped clumsily up to the window-sill with the brooch in its beak and with a raucous "Ta-raah!" was gone.

CHAPTER TWO.   **Curd de Lion.**

Henry? HENRIETTA!" The Twin's mother burst through the door into the playroom like a great gale, flinging Curd onto the floor where Henry, Henrietta and their Animals were sitting.

"My brooch has gone. The precious emerald and diamond silver brooch that Grandmother gave me. It was in my jewellery box before you upset it. Now it's not there. Where is it?" she demanded.

"I don't know," replied Henry, lowering his eyes.

"I didn't take it," added Henrietta.

"This is serious. No one else has been in there," said Mother, "You must know where it is. Unless you find it before your birthday, I'm going to confiscate all your Animals. I'm going to give them to the Charity Shop for children in need. You'll never see them again. And you'll get no presents. No presents! Do you hear?"

"But we didn't hide it, we didn't." they cried.

"You don't care about them anyway," shouted Mother, "look at the way you were treating Curd the Lion just now. Beating him to rags, you were."

"We weren't. He was a dragon," began Henry.

"It was a game," added Henrietta.

"Well, it just isn't good enough," said Mother, "you've got four days to find my brooch, – or ELSE!"

Mother swept out of the room like a vacuum cleaner, sucking the protesting Twins out after her.

As the door closed with a bang, the Animals slowly gathered in shocked

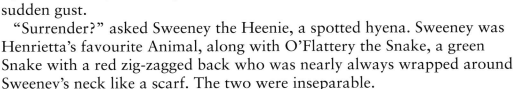

silence around the heap that was
Curd.

"Stand back and give him some
air," said Pilgrim Crow, a black
crow with a tall hat who was
Henry's other Animal and Curd's
best friend. "The poor fellow will
be suffocated."

He leaned over and flapped his
wings in Curd's face.

"I surrender, I surrender,"
squeaked Curd, woken by the
sudden gust.

"Surrender?" asked Sweeney the Heenie, a spotted hyena. Sweeney was
Henrietta's favourite Animal, along with O'Flattery the Snake, a green
Snake with a red zig-zagged back who was nearly always wrapped around
Sweeney's neck like a scarf. The two were inseparable.

Sitting up, Curd rubbed his eyes to make sure he wasn't dreaming. Yes,
he was here, with his Friends, and had not been carried off by that wicked
Black Raven.

"I... I mean... I remember!" stuttered Curd.

"What happened?" said Pilgrim Crow.

"Well... well, it was the Black Raven," gasped Curd, "the Black Raven
who stole... I thought he was a Dragon, but he wasn't... and the jewelled
Brooch, he took it, you know, and he nearly took me... but I escaped...
just!"

"He must be a terrible class of fellow, dis Raven," said Sweeney the
Heenie, "to frighten our man like dat. He looks quite de..."

"Yella fella," said O'Flattery, Sweeney's sly and scheming friend, the
Snake, "and isn't dat a fine ting? Yella, like de cowardy custard dat he is.
To be sure, dat's where he must have gotten his name, Curdy Custard."

An awful hush hovered over the animals, like a great black bird.

"It is not! My name comes from my famous ancestor, Richard Curd-de-
Lion, King of England. Put em up, you Worm, you..." Curd growled, fists
flailing the air.

"Purremup!" he roared, narrowly missing Pilgrim with a left hook.

"I was ony joking, Sor," cried O'Flattery the Snake, slithering behind
Sweeney the Heenie. "T'was merely a jest, honest it was, your honour," he
whimpered, struggling with Sweeney, who was trying to prevent himself
tripping over the quaking snake wriggling between his legs.

"That's enough," said Pilgrim Crow. In his stiff Puritan hat, he was taller than the others, so when he spoke, they listened.

"It is time we addressed ourselves to the problem at hand." He paused, adjusting his tie importantly.

"What problem?" Three voices said as one.

Just then they heard shouting from downstairs, lots of shouting. The Animals crept through the door onto the landing and peered over the edge between the bannisters.

There in the hall stood Mother, wringing her hands together, with Father standing at her shoulder, both arguing with Grandpa and Uncle, who had just arrived from Ireland on his annual visit.

"But you can't take away their Animals," said Grandpa, that's not fair. Look, you can see they're upset."

The Animals looked where he was pointing. There, in the corner, sat Henry and Henrietta, holding each other tight, crying quietly.

"And I don't matter?" shouted Mother. "They can lose my precious brooch, my only family heirloom from my mother's side, and, oh, yes, that doesn't matter? The gift your own wife, rest her soul, gave me when we got engaged. That doesn't matter?"

"Of course it matters," said Grandpa, "but they have told you they don't have the brooch."

"We can all search for it, but you can't go accusing them or punishing them without proof," added Uncle.

"No one else has been in there. The brooch is gone." Mother stamped her foot loudly on the wooden floor and raised her voice even higher. "They must have taken it. And I mean it. Those Animals will go to the charity shop unless they give me back my brooch."

"Wow!" cried Curd.

"Did you hear dat?" said Sweeney, "she really means it. Dat's us she's talkin about. She's goin to give us all away to be sold in a shop!"

"I thought she was joking," said Pilgrim, "but she wouldn't dare argue with Grandpa unless she really meant it."

"We'd be alright den, wouldn't we, Sweeney?" said O'Flattery, "I mean, we're togedder, like, you know."

"Ha!" cried Pilgrim. "She'd wrench you apart just for spite. Look at her! She's really mad."

"In dat case, we've got to do someting, quick," said O'Flattery, "afore she does."

"What?" asked Curd.

"Find it – the brooch – and get it back," said Pilgrim, "before their birth-day."

"When's dat?" asked Sweeney.

"Monday. I heard Dad telling Uncle," said Curd.

"What's today?" asked Pilgrim.

"Tursday, I tink," said O'Flattery, "cos it's Mum's baking day."

"That only leaves four days to get it back from the Great Raven." said Pilgrim.

"Henry and Henrietta – I mean, St. George and St. Georgette – were conquering the Beast, the Dragon," explained Curd, "to save the poor Damsel-in-Distress."

"That's it!" cried Pilgrim Crow, clapping Curd hard on the back, "we'll go on an Adventure, like the brave knights of old, in search of this Great

Raven Dragon Beastie. We'll seek out his lair, conquer him and wrest…"

"Why rest, just when we've found him?" asked Curd.

"Not rest. Wrest. Wrestle from him the jewelled Brooch he has hoarded in his den," said Pilgrim. "But first, we must find where he has gone."

"Home?" suggested Curd, helpfully, "Where he lives."

"An I don't suppose you t'ought to ask him where dat is?" said Sweeney the Heenie, "when you was chattin', like?"

"Er, no," said Curd, "that is, we never quite got around to it…"

"So, no invitations, den," scoffed O'Flattery. "No, 'Come round to my place, why don't you, to see my collection of jewels and stuff'?"

"No, not that, neither," said Curd, "I don't think. Did he say that?"

"Never mind about that," said Pilgrim, "because I know where ravens live. They live up on the moors behind the woods, where the big rocks are. I saw it in Henry's book of Natural History. And we are going to launch our own Great Adventure to rescue Mum's Brooch and save Henry and Henrietta from losing their Best Toys, US!"

"Hooray!" they shouted.

"But we have got no time to lose. We must leave immediately: tonight, after everyone is asleep. And you, Curd the Lion, will be leader of our Adventure, like your famous ancestor, King Curd de Lion."

"Why him?" said O'Flattery the Snake, "Why not Sweeney, here?"

"Because Curd," said Pilgrim Crow, "is the only one who has met the Great Raven, face to face."

"Me, the leader?" asked Curd, trembling with excitement, "Of my own Dragon-hunt? Yippee!"

Even O'Flattery the Snake could not think of argument against this, and he hissed sulkily into a corner.

CHAPTER THREE.   **Nightbears and Ballads.**

Pssst!" O'Flattery's hiss ricocheted around the walls of the Twin's darkened bedroom like a bullet

"Try again," whispered Pilgrim Crow.

"It's no use, he's fast asleep," said O'Flattery, "anyways, it's none of my business if de young tramps doesn't want to come."

"As best hisser, it's your job to wake him," ordered Pilgrim, "so try again."

O'Flattery took another shot at rousing Curd the lion, who was, as always, in bed with Henry. "Hssst! It'sss time!"

Bright searchlights suddenly swept across the walls, as if guards had been alerted by the noise. The animals froze. Only their shadows, casting an animal frieze upon the wall, moved with the lights of the car.

Henry rolled over in his sleep, away from the glare of the lights to reveal Curd the Lion, flattened as he was from being cuddled with great fondness under the sleeping Henry. It was Henry's turn in the top bunk this week. They took turns because they couldn't decide who liked climbing the ladder the most. Curd forgot and climbed straight out, fell from the top bunk and flopped flat onto the floor.

"That's what I call a Lie-on!" chuckled Sweeney the Heenie. A chorus of giggles surrounded Curd the lionskin rug.

"Shush!" whispered Pilgrim Crow. "Check that Henry's still asleep," he added, to give Curd time to regain his composure (which means to pull himself together into his usual shape after being squashed).

Curd padded groggily over to his friend Pilgrim, "I've been having terrible bad dreams in my sleep... Night-bears! Great big horrible Night-bears!"

"Night-bears?" scoffed Sweeney, "Night-bears?"

"Yes," said Curd, "Night-bears. Great big black hairy ones..."

"Never mind them," said Pilgrim impatiently, "You must be brave, because you're the Leader of our Adventure, you know."

"I am?" asked Curd, cheering up, "I'd quite forgot."

"Go on den, lead away." Sweeney gave Curd a kindly push.

"Where to?" asked Curd, as he tripped over O'Flattery's tail, which was all of him apart from his head.

"I'll tell you when we get there," said Pilgrim Crow.

"Right," said Curd looking puzzled, "Let's go then," said Curd the Lion, picking himself up and taking charge of his Very Own Adventure.

The Animals set off, Curd leading the way as leaders do. Pilgrim Crow followed, then Sweeney the Heenie with O'Flattery the Snake wrapped around his neck like a scarf.

They squeezed through the gap in the door.

The Twins always left the door open a crack, to let the Dark out a bit, in case it needed to. The Dark seemed to grow so very quickly with the door shut that they thought that if it were allowed to grow too much, there might not be enough room left for themselves in there as well as the Dark.

As they crossed the landing to the top of the dimly lit staircase, Sweeney darted ahead and bounced down the stairs and across the hall.

Suddenly he almost tripped over a low growl.

"H.... h....hello?" stuttered Sweeney, as the growl grew in the darkness ahead until it filled it completely, squeezing Sweeney back towards the stairs.

Just then a light streamed through the gap under the living room door and flooded the hall floor. There was Ballad, the Twin's red dog, grinning over the edge of his sleeping basket (don't ask why the basket was asleep).

Thump, thump, THUMP... the noise on the other side of the door was getting closer.

"Quick, hide!" croaked Pilgrim. They scuttled for Ballad's basket and dived in just as the door opened and there appeared a monstrous black figure framed against the light. "What is it Ballad?" It was the Twin's father.

Ballad wizzled and whined and wagged his tail.

"Quiet now, boy," grunted Father, as he retreated to the living room, closing the door behind him. The Animals, tucked behind Ballad, heard the sound of footsteps receding, followed by a loud crackling of paper. Father wouldn't be likely to hear them above that noise.

They didn't stop to wonder what he was doing at that time of night, but crept out of Ballad's basket, and tiptoed across the hall to the front door.

"How are we going to turn the handle? It's very stiff," said Pilgrim Crow.

While the animals were arguing about the best way to open the door, Curd found he was staring at O'Flattery the Snake, curled around Sweeney's neck. The more he stared the more he saw a rope wound around a door-knob, with them pulling on the other end, and the door-knob turning as they pulled...

"Pilgrim," Curd whispered into Pilgrim's ear, "I've got an idea."
Pilgrim listened.

"OK," said Curd, "now this is what we'll do."

Soon Curd the Lion was balanced precariously on Sweeney the Heenie's strong shoulders but he was still a foot short of the handle.

"Now O'Flattery, you climb onto my back," said Curd, "reach the handle and wind yourself around it, and pull. I'll pull on you and Sweeney on me and our combined weight will easily turn the handle."

"Or me into two pieces, more like," said O'Flattery, "No t'anks, indeed."

As the animal ladder began to tremble, Pilgrim (for this was the plan

Curd had whispered in his ear) snatched up O'Flattery in his beak and dropped him onto the doorknob. Falling, O'Flattery clung on tight. Curd jumped and grabbed him by the throat, Sweeney jumped and grabbed Curd's hind-legs, Pilgrim grabbed Sweeney and they all pulled hard.

"Yrrr choking me's!" gurgled O'Flattery, as the handle turned and the door flew inwards.

As the animals disentangled themselves, Curd padded over to the half-open door, "Now the danger starts".

"For some," muttered O'Flattery under his breath.

"Watch out now, all of you, for the Great Black Raven and his cronies: Crows, Rooks, and Magpie spies. They have eyes everywhere," whispered Pilgrim, as four pairs of eyes peered out into the darkness; a darkness black as crows.

CHAPTER FOUR.   **The dark side of the Moon.**

It's dark," said Curd the Lion.
"So it is," replied Sweeney the Heenie.

"After you," said Curd politely to no one in particular.

No One in Particular wanted to go first. No One in Particular went first. So Curd stepped out into the inky blackness, pretending he didn't at all mind following No One in Particular, even though HE was leader.

A dull thud, followed by a yelp of pain, came from somewhere out there in the darkness.

"I think Curd's found dat danger of yours, Pilgrim," chuckled O'Flattery the Snake. "Did you find dat danger yet, Curd?" he called out into the night.

Before Curd had time to reply, the moon peeped out from behind its cloud-curtain like some nosey old lady, to reveal him sprawled out on the wet path that glistened like a silver snail trail across the garden to the steps that led into the gloomy wood.

"Typical," grumbled Curd at the moon, "It would come out! Just as I was getting along so well without it."
Pilgrim helped Curd recover his pride, and the Animals set off to climb into the murky wood and the start of their Great Adventure.

They had barely scrambled halfway up the steps when Sweeney the Heenie, seeing the mill-pond in the ever-brightening moonlight, suddenly turned aside and darted towards it, giggling to himself.

CHAPTER 4

"What are you doing?" cried Curd the Lion, as Sweeney stopped at the water's edge.

"Moonraking," shouted Sweeney, gazing at the moon's reflection in the glassy water.

"He's right," said O'Flattery, " the moon IS down there in the water, just like he says."

They all looked. Sure enough, there was a second moon, deep down in the blackness of the pond.

"Is that really another moon down there?" asked Curd the Lion.

"Shhh!" snapped Sweeney, "I'm pondering. How can I ponder when you'se lot keep interrupting me reflections?"

"What's pondering?" asked Curd, not wanting to interrupt it.

"It's what you do by a pond," explained Pilgrim Crow. "It means fishing with your thoughts very deep in the water."

"And if you ponder hard enough," added Sweeney, "you can drag de moon right up to de surface, so de Grand-da said.

"Look, it's getting bigger – it's coming!" Curd cried excitedly.

Four pairs of eyes stared at the moon growing in the water. It was coming closer.

"It works," cried Sweeney, more surprised than anyone, "I'm pondering de moon and it's coming."

The moon grew and grew.

"De moon's a balloon!" Sweeney was agog.

They could make out a face now, and then a basket, swinging and spinning...now under it... now over it... now round about it. A pair of large white gloves and bag-like boots hung from the basket, waving and kicking as the basket spun about. Between the balloon-head and the basket-belly they could see a flame, which roared and flared now and again, illuminating the whole of the balloon from within. The moon was now racing up towards them through the water at a frightening speed.

"It's going to land," Curd stammered, "I... I mean... it's going to burst right out of the water!"

"It can't, can it?" O'Flattery didn't wait to find out, but hid behind Sweeney. Curd covered his eyes.

With a mighty splash, the moon's reflection burst out of the water, drenching them all. As they stood beside the pond, dripping and staring in silent amazement, a voice surfaced with the floundering inflatable.

"I say there, help a fellow out, won't you?"

Sweeney the Heenie and Curd the Lion waded in, each gripped a glove in their jaws, and hauled the great balloon onto dry land. The balloon wobbled, swayed, and righted itself with blast of hot air from its bread-basket that almost lifted the surprised Lion and Hyena into the air.

"Allow me to introduce myself: Professor Ballooonafuss. Professor of Emphatics..."

"What's Emphatics?" asked Curd.

"EmFATics," explained Pilgrim, "makes things FATTER. Wind-bags, balloons, that sort of thing."

"Nothing of the sort," huffed the Balloonafuss. "EMPHATICS, my dear

boy, are like mathematics, but MORE so!" added the Professor grandly, waving his gloves in the air. "With EMPHATICS, you always get your sums right."

"How?" asked Curd. "In mathematics, Henry always gets his sums wrong. He can't count."

"Well, WE have a way around THAT, and no mistake. You don't NEED to count. What counts in EMPHATICS is SIZE. Whatever you say, you emphaSIZE it, see? And SIZE adds STRENGTH. And STRENGTH is MIGHT. And MIGHT is RIGHT! See?"

"But why is might right?" asked Curd, not seeing at all.

"Because, you don't ARGUE with it, do YOU?" roared the Balloonafuss, leaning threateningly over the bewildered companions, "because, if you DO..."

"No, no... we don't." Curd suddenly saw it all too clearly.

"Don't argue," Pilgrim Crow added hastily.

"Well then, if no one disagrees with it, it MUST be right, RIGHT?"

"Right," echoed four voices feebly, frightened that the Fuss might explode in another outburst.

Curd turned to Sweeney and whispered, "Why did you bring him here anyway, Sweeney? I wish you hadn't brought him."

"Brought me? BROUGHT me?" bellowed the Balloonafuss. "Quite the reverse. I brought YOU. I invented you. You are mere figments of my imagination, brought to light, so to speak, by my brilliance. Why, if I went away, you would disappear entirely, don't you see?"

"No we would not! We would still be here!" said Curd.

"Would you indeed?" said the Professor. "If you couldn't see each other, how could you know you were still here?"

Curd thought he knew the answer to this, but couldn't quite put his finger on it.

"We could touch each other," Pilgrim Crow said.

"How touching! And what would be touching what, may I ask? How could you know?" said the Balloonafuss.

"We would remember, from before, when we could see each other," said Sweeney the Heenie.

"Remember? Memory is mistaken identity, that's all. My dear Creatures, just because you LOOK the same as the day before doesn't mean you ARE the same. Why if you were the same you'd be back where you started. Today would be yesterday and then where would you be?" The Professor beamed down on them as he said: "Enough of this idle banter. It's high time I erased you from my sight. Out of sight, out of mind; that's what I say. I might see you again sometime, should I choose to RE-MEMBER you. Ha-ha!"

With that roar of laughter, the great Balloonafuss rose, rocking and swaying, into the night sky and darkness descended into its place once more.

"He certainly gets carried away wid himself, and no mistake," quipped Sweeney.

"Well I never!" huffed Pilgrim Crow as the Balloonafuss disappeared.

"According to him, you never were!" said Sweeney jokingly; then added seriously, "By de way, where are you? It's black as pitch. I can't see a t'ing."

Suddenly four frightened animals fumbled about them for a sign of something certain... for the feel of a friendly face... But would it be a friendly face they felt?

"Are you there?" a voice trembled in the darkness.

"I think I am," another voice replied.

But, what if the Balloonafuss was right? What if what they touched was not a friendly face? What then? What if what they touched was... NOTH-ING? What if the dark really had swallowed their friends, as it seemed to have done? Not one of them dared reach out... just in case.

Each animal sat alone, shivering in the damp, dark night.

The dark was as black as ink. Curd, cold, wet with dew, and miserable, began to think. He tried to think himself warm. It didn't work. So he tried to think bright thoughts to help the day along. He had almost given up when a ray of hope shone into his head.

"INK! That's the answer," he shouted suddenly, "If it rained in the dark, that would be like pouring water into ink. I once saw Henry do this to Dad's ink. Then the dark would get thinner and thinner, like ink. And then we would be able to see through it; and that would be the same as day.

That must be what the dew is for: to wash away the dark, because when you wake up each morning, the dark is gone, and all that is left is the dew on the ground."

Suddenly Curd felt comfortably damp, but perhaps not damp enough. For now he knew that the damper it became, the more quickly would the dew wash away the dark, and the quicker the day would arrive.

And whatever the day brought, even if it was the Great Raven itself, it couldn't be worse than this awful dark.

CHAPTER 5

CHAPTER FIVE.   **Morning Mists.**

Agrey mist floated up out of the inky night. Furtive shadows slunk from one darkness to another like thieves, trying to escape the dawn.

Suddenly a pencil beam of light pierced the gloom and drew a pink rose right under Curd's nose. As the rose grew red apart from its greening leaves Curd saw that its petals were covered in dew-drops.

"It works," he cried, "It works!"

He looked again. In each glistening bead of dew, sat little Curds and Sweeneys and O'Flatterys and Pilgrims. Lots of them.

"Oh dear, Professor Balloonafuss was right," he said, "We are not the same today at all."

"What do you mean?"

Curd looked round. There they were, life-sized – Pilgrim Crow, Sweeney the Heenie, and O'Flattery the Snake, – just like yesterday, each staring at their own little Friends peering out from the jewelled drops.

"We're still here!" The Friends hugged and laughed with happiness.

Then through their chatter Curd thought he heard a little voice, close by.

He peered around until he saw, under the rose, a stripy caterpillar, all orange-yellow and black, hanging upside down by a thread, spinning around and around, singing:

"Busy, busy, busy, busy,
    Spinning makes me dizzy.
    Helter-skelter, helter-skelter,
    Spinning out my winter shelter."

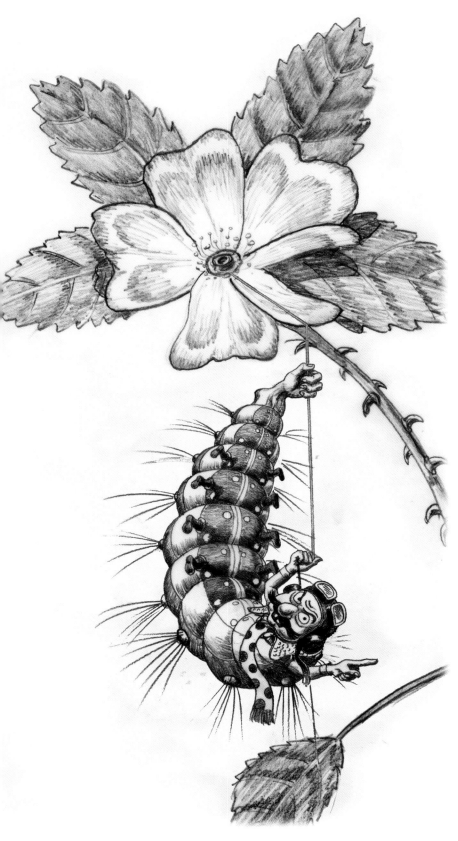

Curd stared in amazement at the little creature, weaving a silken house around itself.

"Oi! What-cha staring at?" said the little voice suddenly.

"Your stripes. They're so bright," said Curd.

"Bird-scarer," said the Caterpillar, "so as not to be eaten."

The Caterpillar waited for another question, but Curd couldn't think of one.

"Why don't you ask me what I am doing?" it said, twisting so that its head was the right way up.

"I'm spinnin' me hangar ready for when I get me wings," it answered. "I'm going to be a pilot next year."

"Excuse

me," said Sweeney, "but you don't look like you could ever fly – not wid all those legs."

"That's because I ain't been to Military Academy yet," said the Caterpillar.

"What's Military Academy?" asked O'Flattery.

"It's Army School where they teaches you to make Feats of Arms and," added the Caterpillar, "if you can do that, why, making Wings of Legs should be as easy as sneezing."

"Are you going to be a butterfly, den?" asked Sweeney the Heenie.

"Butterfly? Bah!" replied the Caterpillar, "I'm going to be a Moth… A Tiger Moth! I'll flutter so loopily no great big bird will ever catch me."

Curd suddenly remembered why they were here: "Have you seen a bird: a Great Raven? He's huge, black…"

"Why yes," said the Caterpillar, "he nearly ate me yesterday. Only I fooled him. I bungeed off of this flower and he got a beakful of petals. See?" He pointed to a slice missing from the rose above him. With that the caterpillar started spinning again, "busy, busy, busy…"

"Which way did he go," asked Sweeney?

"That way," answered the Caterpillar, pointing a little arm out as he span.

"But which way is dat?" asked Sweeney, "you're spinning too fast."

"Not fast enough" replied the Caterpillar, spinning faster, "Not enough time. Snow is in the air. Busy, busy, busy…" He spun faster and faster until his bright black and orangey-yellow stripes turned as white as snow.

"Well, he's no use," grumbled Pilgrim, "Come on! We've no time to lose either, if we're going to save Henry and Henrietta's Birthday Party."

They hurried up the stone steps from the pond to a forest path that wound up the valley towards the moors and their hunt for the beastly Great Raven. The dark trunks of the trees seemed to close in on them like the gigantic bars of a prison. The ground was dappled with light and shade. Even the mist-laden air, streaked like a zebra's coat in the growing sunlight, seemed solid enough to touch.

There was a long drop from the path's edge to the valley bottom, with a silvery stream threading through the leafless woodland.

Pilgrim Crow's sharp eyes noticed a movement in the mist ahead.

"Shh! Freeze!" he wheezed fiercely.

If the magpie had not moved, Pilgrim would never have spotted it, perched on a dead tree across the path ahead, in the uncannily pied light of that morning. They could now make out, above the murmuring of the stream, a muffled chattering that seemed to come from somewhere beyond

the magpie.

"What's that noise?" whispered Curd.

"I don't know," croaked Pilgrim, "but we'll soon find out. It's coming from directly ahead. We'll have to sneak past that magpie."

The four Animals crept forward cautiously whenever the magpie turned away. It seemed to be very keen to join in the whatever-it-was that was going on.

"What do we do now?" asked Sweeney.

31

"O'Flattery could sneak up on it," said Curd.

"Thanks Curd, but we snakes are not as fond of magpies as magpies are of snakes."

The magpie cleared their path by flying away towards the noise.

"Now's our chance," cried Sweeney, as he raced towards the next bend in the path.

He was crouching behind a tree when the others caught up with him, peering intently at the scene beyond.

"Just look at dat, will you now?" he exclaimed.

"Amazing," said Curd.

"How are we going to get past dat lot?" asked Sweeney.

"I'm not!" gasped O'Flattery, imagining how many portions of snake-pie one O'Flattery could make.

Beyond the bend, a horde of chattering and bickering magpies centred upon a circle of magpies on an island in the stream. This was the Great Magpie Moot: annual Parliament of the Magpies.

The assembled magpies were so wrapped up in their wranglings that there seemed a chance of sneaking past. But their path led straight towards the meeting ground.

"I'll scout on ahead," said Pilgrim Crow, and he flew away up the hill. They waited until he returned a few moments later.

"There's a cave up ahead," he crowed excitedly, "and another footpath above it leads up along the valley where we want to go." He flew off again as quickly as he had come.

As they clambered up over the rock-strewn slope, Curd slipped and dislodged a stone, which went clattering down the hill and tripped a shrieking magpie alarm that echoed across the valley. The whole gathering flocked towards them, screaming their blood-curdling war cry: "A pike! A pike! A pike!"

Sweeney scrambled over the ridge leading to the cave mouth, O'Flattery-scarf flying behind, just as the first cohort of magpies reached Curd.

Curd, surrounded by the stabbing pikes and vicious beaks of the mobbing magpies, fought bravely. As he snatched at one with his claws, it would retreat and hover, only to renew its attack, jabbing and stabbing, as soon as he turned to fend off an attack from another direction. Under the hail of blows Curd was compelled to surrender, but not before Sweeney and O'Flattery had made their escape.

Sweeney, carrying O'Flattery, hissing more out of terror than to frighten the magpies, dashed towards the cave-mouth and tumbled headlong down its throat into the darkness. His pursuers ranged themselves across the entrance in a screeching mob, blocking it with a bristling hedge of spears and pikes.

Pilgrim, hearing the commotion, flew back in time to see Sweeney the Heenie and O'Flattery the Snake disappear down the old mine hole, and Curd disappear under a thicket of magpies. He realised it was too late to do anything to save him now from capture.

He flew away, unseen, to try to think of a plan to help him escape.

CHAPTER 6

CHAPTER SIX.   **In the Court of the Pie-Powder.**

As Pilgrim flew away, the thicket of magpies moved like a cumbersome hedgehog down the slope towards the path. The birds half dragged, half carried their helpless prisoner over the rocks.

Muddy and exhausted, Curd stood in the open ground of the Magpie-Moot, encircled by a ring of twenty-two Magpie-Elders.

Facing him sat a group of seven obviously Very Important Pies: three on either side of a central bird, standing grandly behind a low rock that looked remarkably like a writing desk. Curd thought this must be their leader (for it was impossible to tell them apart).

A voice rang out: "Who is this vagabond?"

"Bow," ordered the guard, forcing Curd's head down with the point of a pike, "in the presence of his most Magnanimous Magnificence, his Majesty King Much of a Muchness."

"Let the Trial commence," said the King, putting a white wig on his

head.

"But your Majesty," started Curd.

"No comments," snapped the guard, "and address his Muchness as 'Your Magistery' during the Trial: he's chief Magistrate now."

The first of the six VIPs, acting jointly as the Prosecution, said: "The Court of the Pie-powder is hereby convened, for to try, condemn, and execute sentence against this vagabond."

"What charges are laid against the accused?" asked the King.

"That this vagabond did wilfully and unlawfully wander through and trespass upon the King's Pie-ways," said the second VIP.

"That he be a spy and a pirate," added the third.

"Have you anything to say in your defence?" asked the King.

"Yes, I..."

"M'lud." Curd's speech was cut short by the fourth VIP. "His defence, M'lud, could damage the case for the Prosecution, M'lud."

"So we find him also guilty of 'a-damaging-de-fence', M'lud." continued the fifth.

"And that's an act of wanton vandalism, if ever I heard of one, M'lud." added the sixth.

"Quite reasonable," said the King. "Defence dismissed."

"But your Magistery," pleaded Curd.

"THAT," ordered the King, removing his wig, and staring piercingly at Curd, "concludes the case for the Civil Court."

"Pretty un-civil court, if you ask me," muttered Curd.

"And now we must tackle the more serious charges," added the King, turning away.

"He's putting on his Pious Hat, now," whispered Curd's guard, "which he wears as Archbishop of the Piety."

The King turned back, wearing a tall conical hat with a white circle emblazoned with a strange device.

"You are charged," he announced, conducting the prosecution himself, "with conspiring to spy upon the most Holy Feast of the Epiephany, celebrating the coming of the Great Pie-in-the-Sky, with intent to pirate his most sacred recipe."

"What recipe, your Piety?" asked Curd the Lion.

"What recipe?" scoffed the King, "why, our recipe for Mince-Pies, of course; our most jealously-guarded Secret, passed from generation to generation of Piemen during this very Feast of the Epiephany. How do you plead?"

"Not guilty!" shouted Curd.

A hush fell over the assembly.

"Not guilty?" blurted the King. "But you are FOUND guilty! You can't go spying on the Great Pie-in-the-Sky and hope to get away with it! The Great Pie sees everything. We say you are guilty, and so guilty you are. But we are a just and reasonable King, and will abide by the verdict of the majority. All those in favour of a nice 'guilty' verdict, say 'Pie'!"

A great "Pie!" rose from the basin and bubbled around the lips of the elders.

"Well that, it seems, settles that. Don't you agree?" said the King rubbing his wings together gleefully. Not waiting for Curd's answer, he ordered, "Put him in vagabondage, while I decide upon a Sentence.

CHAPTER SEVEN.   **King Ziggu's Mines.**

Diving headlong into the entrance of the mine, Sweeney the Heenie and O'Flattery the Snake tumbled down and down in an avalanche of tin cans, bottles, cartons and boxes that littered its entrance.

They picked themselves up at the bottom of the slope, breathless and bruised. "At least we escaped dem magpies," said O'Flattery as the last can rattled to a standstill.

They looked back to see the entrance completely blocked. A bristling hedge of magpies, brandishing pikes and spears, taunted them to come out and fight. But strangely none of them came in.

"But it looks like we're trapped," said Sweeney the Heenie, "we can't go back up dere, anyways."

Looking down the tunnel, their eyes strained hard to see in the gloom, and their ears strained hard to shut out the horrible cackling of the birds so that they could hear if anything was moving further on down.

"What's dat smell?" said Sweeney the Heenie.

"It's not de rotten rubbish, for sure," replied O'Flattery the Snake, "It's nastier than dat."

"It's sorta sweet an sickly, like… Shh, O'Flattery, stop scuffling about, I'm trying to t'ink."

"I'm not scuffling," protested O'Flattery the Snake.

The scuffling grew louder. The hackles rose on Sweeney's neck. In that instant he remembered what that smell signified.

"Rats!"

Too late! They were set upon by a hundred scratching claws and snapping jaws. A horde of rats, sharp-clawed and keen-eyed in their murky underworld, attracted to the surface by the noise, had stealthily crept up their familiar runs in the darkness and pounced on the unsuspecting Animals.

One rat grabbed at O'Flattery and pulled. O'Flattery uncoiled and the rat fell over backwards with O'Flattery's tail lashing him. Another grabbed at it and together they began a tug-of-war.

Sweeney lashed out with tooth and claw, snapping and tearing at any within reach. Rats scattered in all directions and scurried back to lick their wounds.

"Surrender!" The Rat-captain's voice rattled tinnily down the tunnel, "Or the Snake gets it."

Sweeney stopped fighting. He climbed down from the mound of battered rats, and advanced upon the Rat-captain, snarling, "Alright, Rat; I surrender."

The rats fell over themselves to get away as he advanced, and the Rat-captain himself retreated behind O'Flattery to ensure Sweeney understood his threat: "Bind him."

The rats dithered, pushing and shoving one another forward in their haste not to be the first to try.

"No tricks, mind," said the Captain, tightening his grip on O'Flattery. A couple of rats held the noose, while two more grabbed his forepaws, and dug their sharp little claws into his fur. They slipped the noose quickly over his head. Triumphant now, they turned to O'Flattery.

"Noose him," ordered the Captain. As they dropped the noose over O'Flattery's head, it fell straight to the floor.

"But he's got no neck, sir!" "He's all neck, sir."

After several attempts, they managed to tighten the noose somewhere below his head.

"Right, lets go," ordered the Rat-captain, and they set off.

Down tunnel after tunnel they were dragged, ever deeper into the bowels of the earth. The walls and roofs of the tunnels dripped continuously as they splashed at first, then puddled, and eventually waded waist-deep through the slimy ooze of the deepest part of the rat-realm.

The air was thick with the stench of rats. The torches of the rat-guards nearly guttered out in the foul air, yet their captors goaded the two Animals on at a breathless pace.

At last they ascended to a drier, though no less smelly, part of the cave system. Turning a corner, they entered a large dome-roofed cavern, spangled with many torches. In the eerie light, the cavern floor was criss-crossed by the flickering shadows of hundreds of rats running their errands to and from distant parts of the old mine workings. It was a humming ratropolis.

In the centre of this hall, enthroned upon a tattered old armchair set on a small stepped pyramid, was an enormous and vicious looking rat, with a crown upon his head.

"Bejapes! I bet dat's de King Rat!" said Sweeney. "I'm glad I didn't have to fight him at de mine entrance."

"Grovel, dog, before King Ziggu, Lord of the Underworld," ordered the Rat-captain, shoving him hard in the back as another rat tripped him

up. They threw O'Flattery to the ground ahead of Sweeney, and one rat pounced on him to pin him down; as if he needed to. O'Flattery did not move.

Sweeney, however, struggled to his feet and stood his ground defiantly as Ziggu, the monstrous Rat-king, rose to his feet, descended the seven steps of his throne, and advanced toward him.

Sweeney flinched for an instant as the rat pointed his finger directly at him and said in a cold voice: "How dare you barge into the realm of Ziggu-Rat, and assault my people?"

"Sure, it was we who was attacked first," said Sweeney.

"You've caused serious damage to our crops," said the King.

"What crops?" asked Sweeney.

"The crops in the mine entrance, that you trampled on and mowed down like a vandal." The King was indignant.

"Crops indeed. Rubbish, it was, so!" Sweeney laughed.

"Cheeky dog!" said King Ziggu. "What sort of dog are you, anyway? I've never seen a dog like you before."

"I'm not a dog," giggled Sweeney.

"I'll have no more of that giggling," growled the Rat-king.

"But I can't help it," sniggered Sweeney, "it's in-bred."

"I don't care if it's in bread and butter, I'll have no more of it," growled King Ziggu, "What are you then, if you're not a dog?"

"I'm a Heenie… Sweeney de Heenie, Sor."

"You'll soon be sore if don't stop that infernal giggling. Why did you invade my realm?"

"We didn't; we was chased in by dem magpies," replied Sweeney.

"Chased, eh?" said the King, sniffing a profit. "Hmmm. Maybe the magpies will pay to get them back. Send some messengers to the Magpie-Moot and get the best bounty you can for them."

The King turned and climbed back to his throne. Sweeney and O'Flattery were left, bound, at the foot of the steps.

"How do you t'ink we're going to get out of dis mess," O'Flattery asked Sweeney.

"I could rhyme dem to death, as dey do Irish rats," said Sweeney, "let me t'ink now…"And so he began:

"Ahem.

Dere was once a fine Rat,
Wid a fuzzy felt Hat.
Wid a Tie dat was pied,
An' a Monocled eye,

Dat fine tatty Rat,
Stood on his door mat,
An' a 'Welcome' was written on dat."

The Rats were looking at each other, nonplussed, pleased even. One or two started to clap.
Sweeney smiled and went on:

"Den along came a Cat.
A chattery Cat,
Wid a battery-bat
Came, a rat-a-tat, tat,
A rat-a-tat, tat, tat-tat!

"What's dat rat-a-tat, tat?"
Said de fat tatty Rat,
"Not dat Cat wid de Bat?
Not dat Cat? Oh my Hat – not Dat?"

But de chattery Cat
Soon arrived, for all dat,
Wid his battery-bat,
Wid his rat-a-tat, tat;
And he sat on de Rat for a chat.

De chat of de Cat,
About dis an' dat,
Was impressed on de Rat
Wid de fuzzy felt Hat
By de rat-a-tat, tat,
Of de battery-bat;
Was impressed on de Rat wid de Bat.

Said de Cat: "Dat's my mat
On which you are sat,
You naughty fat Rat
Wid you're fuzzy felt hat.
Tut-tut, tatty Rat, none of dat!"

So he left him like dat,
Did de chattery Cat,
Wid his battery Bat;
Wid a rat-a-tat, tat,
He left him like dat:
A flat battered Rat on de Mat!"

The rats were looking queasy now. Some were rolling their eyes, others clutching their stomachs.

"I t'ink it's workin'," whispered O'Flattery the Snake, "keep goin' now…"

"Dat's it," replied Sweeney, "Dat's de end."

"Say it again, quick," said O'Flattery, "dey're recovering, hurry!"

Suddenly there was a rumbling and a murmering and a squeaking and a roaring and a panic of rats burst into the hall, overrunning the steps, upsetting the Great Throne and even King Ziggu himself, as they tumbled over one another in their haste to flee.

"What's going on?" screamed Ziggu at the fleeing horde. "Stop! Stop, I tell you," he yelled, until he too was swept bodily out of the Hall in the crush.

Sweeney and O'Flattery found themselves alone in the Great Chamber. As the screams and scufflings of the retreating rats died away, they heard the clod, clod, clod, of heavy footsteps approaching the Cavern from the other direction.

"I think it's time we went," said O'Flattery, "Curd and Pilgrim will be gettin' worried about us, so dey will."

"Curd's a prisoner, you eejit! Of dem Magpies. And anyways, where'd we go to?" asked Sweeney. "That way?" He pointed in the direction of the rats.

"Well, I don't like de sound o' dem footsteps," said O'Flattery, "not one bit."

"Whatever's making dat noise, it can't be worse dan dem horrible rats," said Sweeney, "I t'ink I'd rather take me chance with dat whatever it is. Let's just wait and see, now."

Like a slow bass-drum roll, the noise grew louder.

"Dey've arrived! Two T'umpin Great Whatever-it-ises! Look, I'm off." O'Flattery wriggled and squirmed, trying to get out of his bonds.

Clump, clump, clump. Two huge figures stamped into view, each step shaking the floor like a pile-driver. They turned their craggy stone heads this way and that, sniffing the air with their gigantic noses, peering about

with beady deep-set eyes.

"But what's this?" said the first, tall, skinny one, waving a miner's lamp swinging on the end of a long pole, so close to Sweeney and O'Flattery that their shadows rose up on the opposite wall like ghouls.

"A spotty rat and a worm," said the other, short and squat, crunching the ground with his heavy pick as he stamped up and peered at them closely, as if he needed glasses.

Both wore old, collarless, shirts and ragged trousers held up with braces, tied at the ankles with rusty bicycle-clips.

"I'm no rat," protested Sweeney, "I'm a hyena, Sweeney de Heenie, Sors, at your service," replied Sweeney, bowing to their rescuers, "and dis here is O'Flattery de Snake."

"That so?" Said the tall one. "Then what are you doing down here with little stinkers, eh?"

"We was captured, Sor," said Sweeney.

"We was just working out how to escape," added O'Flattery.

"We'd nearly succeeded in escapin', you mean," added Sweeney, "but you beat us to it."

"Really? Well, I'm Nook!" said the tall one, introducing himself and holding out a moss-covered cudgel of a hand.

"And Cranny!" His chuckle shook the walls around the Great Chamber like an earthquake.

"How do you do?" said Sweeney and O'Flattery together.

"The better for getting out of here, away from this stench," said Nook. "Come on."

Nook and Cranny led Sweeney and O'Flattery out of the cavern of the rats, and down endless tunnels with innumerable turns. Nook's lamp bathed the stark mine-walls in a warm friendly light. They noticed that the

air, strangely, was becoming fresher, smelling less and less, the floor, drier, and the walls were no longer dripping.

"Here we are then," said Nook. They entered a homely chamber with straw-covered stone seats, a great slate table and a cosy fire glowing in the hearth.

Shutting the stone door behind firmly them, Cranny sat them down, while Nook hung his lamp from a hook in the ceiling.

"How did you get into such a mess?" he asked.

"Well, we are on an Adventure," said Sweeney, "to save Henry and Henrietta from losing deir birthday presents."

"What? No presents on their birthday?" said Cranny. "Unheard of."

"And to save us too, from de Shops," added O'Flattery. "Mum's goin' to sell us off."

"Sell you off... to Strangers?" asked Nook. "What have you done?"

"Not us. Mum tinks de Twins took her favourite Brooch and won't give it back," said Sweeney.

"But they can't, see. Because He took it..."

"Who?" asked Cranny.

"De Great Raven," said O'Flattery. "We've got to find where he lives to

44

get de stolen jewelled Brooch back before deir Birthday. But we haven't a clue where he lives."

"Old Corbie," nodded Nook.

"Who?" asked O'Flattery the Snake.

"Old Corbie. He's is the one you call the Great Raven," explained Nook. "He lives way out in the Back of Beyond. I think you had best go and visit Queen Mumbie-Bumbee. Her bee-scouts rove all over the land in search of nectar. She's his sworn enemy so will know just where or how to find him. I am sure she'll tell you if you tell her that we sent you."

Just then Cranny brought a plate piled high with rock cakes, saying, "She gives us the honey for our rock cakes."

"Er, t'anks." But the rock cake wasn't as bad as it sounded. It was a nutty sort of cake glued with honey. In fact, so not bad that it wasn't until several cakes later that Sweeney managed to find his voice again: "if we find dis Mr Old Corbie, do you t'ink he'll mind our askin' for our Brooch back, Mr Cranny, Sor?"

"Oh no, you mustn't ask him. You'll just have to look around and find it for yourselves when you get there," answered Cranny.

"Don't you t'ink he'll mind us lookin' around, den, don't you?" piped up O'Flattery.

"Of course he'll mind. He'll do his best to stop you," replied Cranny, "so you'd better watch out. The two of you are hardly a match for Old Corbie, you know."

"Begob, I forgot!" cried Sweeney. "Our friend, Curd de Lion! He was captured by dem Magpies what was chasin' us. We got to hurry. We got to rescue him quick."

"You mean you've got a friend with you? Captured by the Magpies?" said Cranny.

"Not one, two. Pilgrim Crow too. Ony he wasn't captured. He escaped," said O'Flattery.

"Hold on now," said Nook. "You've got to get out of this cave first. So Cranny will take you a safe exit, away from the rats, and I'll go and look for Curd. When I find him, I'll bring him along to that exit. So when you get there, just wait, right?"

"Anyt'ing you say, Sor," said Sweeney, "we'll be dere, sure as mustard."

"Right," said O'Flattery, "right as mustard."

"Are you sure?" said Sweeney.

"I'm off," said Nook, and he was. They watched his lantern disappear down one of the long passages leading from the room.

At that moment there was a loud hammering on the door Cranny had shut behind them. "Drat! Those rats are here," he growled, "let's go."

CHAPTER 8

CHAPTER EIGHT.   **Escapades.**

Pilgrim fled the magpie-mob. "I'll never be able to rescue Curd with so many Magpies all around," he thought.

As he flew, as fast as his whirring wings would take him away from those spiky Pies, his brain was whirring too. How can you frighten off those Magpies, Pilgrim Crow? You can't. They're too big and too many. Well, can you divert them away to let Curd escape? What with? I don't know. You tell me. What do they like most? I've no idea, but I do know what they don't like. What's that? They don't like dogs. Dogs chase them. So they do. Ballad does, partridges anyway. He might like chasing Magpies too. So let's get Ballad, then. Right, let's get Ballad. But will he listen to us? We'll have to bluff him.

By this time he was home again. He strutted up to Ballad, put his fingers to his collar like lawyers do and said in his gruffest croak: "Ok, Ballad. The Game's up!"

"Game? Partridges?" woofed Ballad, "where?"

"No, Henry and Henrietta's birthday party game, " Pilgrim replied, "unless you come to the rescue."

"In that case Pilgrim," woofed Ballad, "Lead on!"

"But I haven't brought a lead," said Pilgrim, "can't you go without one?"

"Silly bird," barked Ballad, "I meant, show me the way!"

"Oh, that," said Pilgrim, feeling foolish. "Follow me!," he cawed and flew as fast as fast can be. Ballad ran after him, as fast as dogs can, baying loudly.

"Shut up," cawed Pilgrim, trying to be heard over the dog's howls. "They'll hear you a mile off and our ambush will be ruined."

"Ambush? I love ambushes," woofed Ballad, "I'm an expert creeper. I'm a pointer."

I knew there had to be some point ter him, groaned Pilgrim under his breath as the two of them ran and flew without a bark or hoot up the glen towards the Magpie Moot.

The magpie-mob was clapping loudly for his Majesty King Much of a Muchness.

"The Sentence I pronounce…" started the pompous Pie-King.

He was cut short by a blast from the Pied piper's trumpet announcing the arrival of "messengers from his Highness King Ziggu-Rat of Rattendom". The rat delegation was met with silence and suspicious glances.

"Though we have long been at war," began their orator, "our high King, Ziggu, and your own King Much have shaken hands and are now at peace…"

"Yes, get on with it," scowled King Much of a Muchness, who hated all speeches other than his own, "get on with it."

"Well, it's like this, your Majesty," continued the orator. "We captured the two that escaped from your troops and, well, for a small fee…"

Curd learned from the bickering over the 'price on their heads' that Sweeney and O'Flattery had been captured by the rats, who intended to sell them to the magpies for a whole pile of mince pies.

Their endless haggling over exactly how many mince-pies hyenas and snakes were worth was suddenly interrupted by a cry of alarm.

A huge dog came bounding and leaping, barking and yelping, into the centre of the gathering, scattering birds and rats helter-skelter, squawking and squealing, as it charged around in circles gleefully snapping at anything coming within reach, wreaking havoc wherever it ran.

It was Ballad! Curd had never been so glad to see the Twin's foolish dog, now tearing around like a Catherine wheel, exploding a trail of feathers as he went.

"How did he get here?" asked Curd as his guards fled the rampaging dog.

"I brought him." It was Pilgrim "Quick, turn around and I'll untie your knots."

"Bravo," shouted Curd. "Well done Pilgrim, that was clever thinking."

"Shut up you fool, they'll hear you," said Pilgrim.

"They have," said Curd. "Run!"

Two magpies had evaded Ballad's wild antics and were flying directly towards them.

"Woops, too late," said Curd. "Make out like we're surrendering. When they put their pikes down to tie us up, watch for my signal and grab a pike."

"What signal?" said Pilgrim as he raised his wings in surrender.

The magpies landed beside them. The first put his pike down and picked up the twine dropped by Pilgrim. "Turn around," he ordered.

Just as he was turning Curd looked back behind the magpies and yelled, "Yikes, the dog!" as he ducked down, holding up a paw to cover his head.

Both Magpies looked round. Curd leaped onto the armed Magpie and bit his pike-wing so hard that he dropped it. Pilgrim snatched up the other pike and jabbed the unarmed Magpie in the chest.

While he was still hopping up and down with pain, crying "My wing, my wing, I think it's broke," Curd jumped down and snatched up his pike and jabbed him hard in the foot. The magpie was hopping round on one leg now, grabbing his foot then his wing, howling, until he lost his balance and fell over.

Pilgrim pushed the other Magpie with the point of the pike back until he tripped over his fallen comrade. Curd grabbed the twine and tied their feet together, so that neither could get up without knocking the other over.

"Let's go." As Curd and Pilgrim raced towards a rickety wooden bridge that crossed the stream ahead, more magpies caught up with them and they were attacked from all sides.

Fighting fiercely, Curd could make out now, through the flurry of feathers, a hideous swarthy ragged Hag on the bridge ahead, squinting up at them as she leaned over the water, was washing a bundle of filthy old clothing in the rushing stream.

The Hag rose to her feet with a raucous cackle, and clawed the air with her crooked fingers, creating such a terrifying spectre that the attacking magpies turned and fled. The animals stood rooted to the spot.

"Nasty chattering things, magpies. Eh, me dears?" said the Hag in a thin high voice. "I soon got rid of them for you though, didn't I, me dears?"

She leaned towards them, peering over her long beaky nose, scrutinising them as a butcher might a piece of meat; "Come along, me dears. I'll help you across."

She reached out a scrawny black hand. Neither moved.

"Don't be frightened, me dears. I wouldn't have chased them nasty Magpies off if I was going to hurt you, now would I, me dears?" She smiled, revealing hard toothless gums.

"I'm Mother Beanie, me dears, the old Washer at the Ford. And this is how I makes me living." She gathered her bundle of rags into an old wicker basket. "And that's me cosy house, me dears, where you can rest your little selves," she added, pointing to a half-ruined shed on the far bank of the stream.

She crooned and cajoled them into a false sense of security, in spite of her appearance. "Take me hand, me dears, and form a chain. It be safer that way, with the waters running so high today."

Seeing no other way across the stream, Curd reluctantly took the Hag's hand. Pilgrim Crow took Curd's, more to reassure him than because he needed to.

Curd the Lion stepped carefully onto the flooded bridge. The water swept around his legs, threatening to carry him away, but the Hag's hand held him firm.

"And what brings such gentlefolk as yourselves out into this wilderness, me dears?" asked Mother Beanie, as Curd edged slowly across the bridge, leaning against the weight of water sweeping around his ankles.

Curd, holding the Hag's hand as tightly as she held his, blurted: "Oh, we're on an Adventure, like the knights of old, and we're going to rescue Mum's jewelled Brooch, stolen by the wicked Great Raven."

"Really? With such beastly creatures as them magpies about, my advice is to give up such folly and go back to your comfy little home, me dears." crowed the Hag.

"No, no… We couldn't do that! We must get it back before Henry and Henrietta's birthday on Monday."

"I see. Well, if I can't persuade you to turn back…" began Mother Beanie the Hag.

"No. Nothing will stop us," asserted Curd bravely.

"Nothing?" asked Mother Beanie, "not THIS?"

The Hag jerked her hand round hard, pitching Curd into the raging torrent. Pilgrim, caught off-balance, was unable to catch him, and Curd was swept away towards the thundering waterfall of the weir below the pond.

"KAARK, KAARK!" A huge grey heron flapping low over the water collided heavily with the Hag.

"Clumsy oaf!" squawked Mother Beanie, "watch where you're flying," as she clung to him, scrabbling for a foothold on the bridge.

"You've no right blocking river-traffic," shouted the Heron, "It's my right-of-way," as he wrestled with her," and I'm in a hurry. Got to find a little Lion thing, called Curd. Got to rescue him from a bunch of magpies."

"Ha! You're too late!" cackled the Hag as she floundered on the bridge. "He's gone fishing downstream. Look!"

The heron saw Curd's little form tossing in the waves as he was swept away. The heron cried, "Enough, foul Hag!" and his bill skewered her thick ragged clothing like a fish.

She wriggled free of his embrace and, assuming the form of a black shaggy-feathered bird, flopped clumsily up into the air and away through the trees.

Curd somersaulted and spun helplessly in the powerful current that dragged him towards the weir. Pilgrim watched helplessly as he flew along the bank, trying to keep up.

"Help," cried Curd, as his head bobbed up, only to swallow a mouthful of the brown turbid water. "I'be drowding," he bubbled, underwater, as his paws waved in the air.

The heron flapped down stream, arching his great wings so low over the water that their tips touched the surface as he flew down to the weir. He landed in the fast-flowing but shallow water of the weir's edge and stood poised like a spear-fisherman about to strike.

As Curd was swept towards him, the heron plucked him out by a hind-foot just before he went over the fall. He strode slowly and deliberately towards the further bank, holding the limp and dripping Lion upside down in his long beak.

Pilgrim fluttered over to join them as the heron clumsily deposited Curd on his head on the bank, forcing out a gush of the water he had swallowed.

"Are you alright?" Pilgrim wrung his hands together with worry as Curd wrung out his sodden tail.

"Just give him a minute or two to get his wind back," chuckled the heron, as Curd burped for the third time. "Another minute and you'd have been drowned, for sure. Come along now, I'll take you to your friends."

"You know them?" asked Pilgrim in surprise.

"Know them? Oh, in a manner of speaking. I do know where they are."
"How's that?" asked Pilgrim Crow.
"Well, it's like this...." He stalked off up the hill with Pilgrim Crow, chatting the sort of flighty chat birds of a feather keep to themselves. Curd, who was still a little groggy, trotted a short way behind.

Back in Nook and Cranny's cavern, a loud hammering on the door announced the arrival of the rats.

Cranny doused the fire, and the three of them set off at a trot, leaving the scuffling and hammering of the rats behind.

"That door should hold them for a while," said Cranny, grabbing a lantern.

After a few minutes' climb, they heard a rumbling crash behind them, followed by a chorus of squeals.

"There goes our door," said Cranny. "Hurry now. They'll soon catch up."

Cranny led the way, his heavy footsteps resounding in the narrow tunnel. Sweeney the Heenie hurried along behind, urged on by O'Flattery the Snake, who was covering his back. As the scuffles and cries grew closer, they could see the flickering firebrands of the leading rats in the distance.

"Not far to go now," said Cranny.

Above the squeals and shouts of the rats they could now make out the voice of King Ziggu shouting orders to his troops. The rats rushed forward in one final spurt which carried the leading ones past Cranny before he could go back to defend the animals.

An avalanche of rats swept against the firm trunks of his legs as he turned to face them. He laid about him with blows so ferocious that rats were scythed down like ears of wheat. But still they kept coming.

Sweeney, hampered by O'Flattery about his neck, failed to see two rats sneaking up behind him. They grabbed O'Flattery's head and tail, and pulled on either end as if on a rope. Choking and spluttering, Sweeney faced the onslaught of three more rats.

Suddenly Cranny was there, pushing aside the rats and ushering Sweeney and O'Flattery before him to the base of a mineshaft, while using his bulk to block the rats behind.

"Here we are," he shouted, "your friends will be along shortly, if I know Nook."

He marched back, his flailing arms and lantern driving the rats before him like field mice before a combine-harvester.

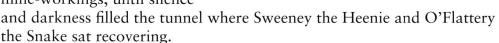

The din of battle slowly receded with the light of Cranny's lamp into the depths of the mine-workings, until silence and darkness filled the tunnel where Sweeney the Heenie and O'Flattery the Snake sat recovering.

As their eyes grew used to the darkness after the bright light of Cranny's lamp, they realised there was still some light coming from somewhere.

They looked up and saw a shaft of light streaming from above. The walls of the mine-shaft were smooth, unassailable.

"We can't go back in de dark, and we can't climb dat shaft," said Sweeney, "so we're stuck here, now. Curd and Pilgrim should come along soon to get us out of here."

Sweeney and O'Flattery waited and waited. It seemed to O'Flattery that they had been an awfully long time at the bottom of the shaft.

"I hope they're alright,"

"Why should we care?" said O'Flattery the Snake, "dey haven't a clue where to go next. We do. We know dat we got to go to Queen Mumbie-Bumbee's and she'll direct us to Old Corbie's hideout and den we'll get de

Brooch back and den we'll be de heroes. We can go it alone."

"But you heard what Cranny said, 'you two are no match for Old Corbie', he said," said Sweeney.

"Well, maybe so. But why should we always have to follow dat dratted Lion? Dat's what I'm saying," grumbled O'Flattery.

Just then a strange head popped over the rim of the shaft and a crackly voice cried out: "You there!"

Startled, they didn't know what to make of this. After a moment's thought, O'Flattery said, "No one here, I'm afraid."

"Come along now, me dears," croaked the voice, "we're all on the same side, aren't we, me dears."

"Which side?" replied Sweeney, "from here it looks like we're on de inside, and you're on de outside."

"So you ARE there, then," croaked the voice.

"Alright, so we are. But how do we get out?" asked Sweeney the Heenie.

"Easy, me dears. You just follows me directions," replied the voice. "I'm Mother Beanie, me dears: and I just met your friends along the way, as it happens."

"No friends of ours," muttered O'Flattery, "dat Curdy Custard don't deserve to be a leader, no more'n our Sweeney de Heenie, here."

"Really, me dears? Well, in that case," replied the cunning Hag, "I'll get directly to the point. I couldn't help overhearing your little conversation just now, about going to Queen Mumbe Bumbie's to find out from her how to find the way to Old Corbie's. But I has the Secret."

"What Secret?" asked O'Flattery, the Snake, his scales prickling with excitement.

"I knows where to find the Brooch you're looking for. But big secrets can only be told to great Leaders. Now if you was to be Leaders, well then, I could tell you. But seeing as…"

"But we are," interrupted O'Flattery, "dat is, we will be," he continued, his brain working furiously, "…with de SECRET!" he added, triumphantly.

"But you must agree to fetch me a little something in return. Stolen goods, it is: stolen from Old Corbie, I might add," chuckled Mother Beanie, the Old Hag. "It's just a little old cup. Just a keepsake given a long long time ago, by a saintly old fellow, for saving his life once upon a time."

"But why would he give Old Corbie a cup?" asked O'Flattery.

"In thanksgiving. Call it a Holy Relic, if you like," answered Mother Beanie, "It is dear to me but a horrid Bee bamboozled me out of it and I want it back. I'll tell you where to find the jewelled Brooch if you get it back for me."

"You mean it was you dat stole da Brooch? I t'ought it was Old Corbie, da Great Raven who done it?" said O'Flattery.

"So it was. Silly of me. But I knows him well," replied Mother Beanie. "I does his laundry. Have done for so long now I forget myself sometimes."

"Right den, it's a deal," said Sweeney, not at all sure what he was agreeing to, "we'll get dat Cup if we can find it – if you'll tell us where de Brooch is hid."

Mother Beanie leaned low into the well's mouth and whispered confidentially down its throat: "This certain Queen Mumbie - a certain thief, she is - has this cup – Old Corbie's Cup - in her chamber. Now you fetch it along and then I'll come by and by and when we next meet you'll give me the Cup and I'll tell you where the Brooch is hid, and we'll all be happy, then, won't we, me dears?"

"Ok, we'll get de Cup," said Sweeney the Heenie, "now tell us where de Brooch is hid."

"Well, it's like this," said Mother Beanie, "where the sun shines through the hole in the Stone on midwinter's day, that's where the Jewel is hidden."

"What stone?"

"The Corbie Stone, of course," laughed Mother Beanie.

"But where's that?"

"That's a Secret not to be told until we meet again," she continued softly. "Now you won't forget me Cup, will you, me dears?"

"Of course not," said Sweeney, "but how do we recognise it? Everyone has lots of cups."

"Not like this one. This one has a big chip, like a bite out of it. And there's a ring around it just below the rim. It's special. Queen Mumbie keeps it in a special place."

"What's so special about an old cracked cup?" asked O'Flattery.

"What's so special about an old Brooch?" replied Mother Beanie.

"Dat Brooch is Mum's favourite," answered Sweeney.

"And that Cup is mine… I mean, Old Corbie's favourite," replied Mother Beanie. "Everything has value to someone, you know."

"Yeah, but a Cup?" O'Flattery asked, looking up. Mother Beanie was gone! "Hoi! What about gettin' us out of here?" he shouted.

There was no reply. Sweeney and O'Flattery were left alone with their thoughts. A scheme began to push all other thoughts out of O'Flattery's head. It was the score he had to settle with Curd and Pilgrim for nearly throttling him on the door-knob. And he now knew exactly how to settle it.

Sweeney for Leader! Sweeney was brave; he had fought off de rats. Sweeney was clever; he could make up poems. Above all, Sweeney listened to him, O'Flattery. So went O'Flattery's thoughts. Yes, Lions had had it too good for far too long. Hyenas had always had a bad press. Yes, Hyena for de King of Beasts! Nobody would go treading on a Snake's dignity anymore. O'Flattery for chamberlain, chief councillor and mentor to his majesty. We'll know de Secret when we give Mudder Beanie de cracked Cup, and den no one else will know, will dey? Unless Sweeney becomes de Leader. And when Sweeney becomes Chief, I'll be his necker-Chief!"

The sun was setting as the heron peered into the darkness of the mine shaft.

"Is that you?" came a familiar voice from the bottom of the pit.

"Who?" croaked Pilgrim.

To Sweeney and O'Flattery the croaking voice was that of old Pilgrim Crow, but the long neck and beak silhouetted against the sky were not. Not a sound issued from the base of the shaft.

"Ha, ha. Yes, it's us!" chuckled Pilgrim as he too looked down.

"Ha, ha." The unmistakeable voice of O'Flattery echoed hollowly from the pit. "Ha-ha. Very amusing."

"Heron, here, who rescued us, is going to stretch his neck down and grab you, O'Flattery," said Pilgrim. "You, Sweeney, climb the pair of them."

The heron craned his neck down the shaft and grabbed O'Flattery who, with little choice, had stretched up to reach him. Soon Sweeney was panting on the grass at the top of the shaft.

As the shades of evening drew in, the heron drew O'Flattery out of the

shaft and laid him on the ground beside Sweeney.

"I'd better be getting along now, it's my suppertime, you know," laughed the heron, winking wickedly at O'Flattery, who shrunk sheepishly behind Sweeney.

The heron took to his great wings, and flapped lazily away, guffawing into the gathering gloom.

CHAPTER NINE.   **The Flitting.**

As they watched the heron disappear into the grey evening, O'Flattery turned to Sweeney and whispered: "Don't forget what I told you."

"Pilgrim," asked Curd, "what was Heron telling you just now, as we were coming here?"

"He said that we must go north along this path through Birkwood to find Queen Mumbie-Bumbee. She'll give us shelter and guide us on our way. She lives under an ancient Hawthorn tree, and always leaves a lantern outside for her returning children. We must look for that lamp."

O'Flattery nudged Sweeney: "You hear dat? Queen Mumbie!"

The four Adventurers set off along the path between the birch trees in cheerful expectation of Mumbie's hospitality, and told each other of their various adventures as they went.

When Pilgrim told of Curd's dunking in the stream at the hands of the old Hag, Mother Beanie, Curd blushed with embarrassment from head to tail. His yellow coat glowed a golden red, rivalling the sunset for brightness.

The sunset purpled into night. The Adventurers trudged through the leafless birch trees swaying gracefully in the night breeze like silver sylphs. Occasionally obscured by wisps of cloud, the moon shone hard and cold for the most part in a clear, starry sky.

The Animals had to keep on the move to keep warm, especially Curd, still damp from his soaking that afternoon. The leaf litter and grasses crunched underfoot; their edges shone with a crystalline brilliance. It was starting to freeze.

Curd looked up through the trees to the starlit dome of the sky, wishing he had a nice warm blanket to curl up in. It seemed that the cold came from those very stars, which glinted so like the frost on the leaves.

Perhaps, he thought, the clouds wrapped their blanket round the earth to keep it warm and protect it from the cold glare of the stars. Curd longed for some clouds to cover the sky, even if it meant he couldn't see. He had forgotten his fright of the previous night.

As he stared at the stars glimmering between the silver trunks of the trees and their frost-rimed branches, it seemed to his fancy that they were moving.

"Isn't it funny," said Curd, rubbing his eyes in disbelief, "how the light plays tricks on your eyes. The stars seem to be moving."

"Don't be silly, Curd," said Pilgrim, "it's you who are moving."

But the others, who had been busy looking out for the light of Mumbie's house, now looked up at the stars. As they looked harder, it began to seem as if the stars were moving. They WERE moving! Now floating, now flitting; sometimes shooting about like little fireworks; sometimes suspended in perfect stillness, staring menacingly at the little band of travellers.

"That's strange," said Pilgrim Crow, "What the...!"

A tiny light whooshed past his head and away, to lose itself among the twinkling stars. The strange lights flitted among the trees like little ghosts, daring closer, whizzing faster, round and round the animals, making them feel giddy as they tried to follow their comings and goings.

"Go away!" shouted Curd, his head spinning, "Stop it! You're making my head spin."

"I can't stop dem!" puffed Sweeney, snatching at the flitting lights swarming like angry gnats around them, "dey're too quick."

"Hide!" cried O'Flattery, ducking under Sweeney's ear.

"Where?" snapped Sweeney, his jaws clapping empty air as he leaped around in circles trying to catch the little demons. "I can't see a ting! Dey're blindin' me."

The animals raced on, trying to avoid the ghastly lights. But they couldn't! Desperately trying to escape the whizzing whirligigs about their heads they lost all sense of direction. The whole world seemed to be a topsy-turvy tumbrel – spinning with light.

"Look! There's Mumbie's house," Pilgrim shouted: "It must be, surely?"

In the distance ahead of them glowed the steady warm light of Queen Mumbie's door lantern, just as Heron had described it. Trying to ignore the wild lights flashing all around, the Animals rushed towards that strong friendly beam. They could make out the shape of the lantern, now, swaying gently back and forth.

"Lookout! Ieee!" Curd fell forward into empty space, and a screech followed him.

It stopped them dead.

"Who turned de lights out?" shouted Sweeney. The scudding lights whirled skywards as if sucked up by a tornado and the air around them choked with blackness.

"Don't move anyone," said Curd, "I think I've fallen into something."

"Where are you?" said O'Flattery, "We can't see a t'ing."

"I'm down here, clinging to a rock, I think," said Curd. "I can't see either."

Suddenly the darkness exploded.

Sweeney, O'Flattery and Pilgrim were crushed under the weight of a blinding light, pulsating in their eyes and they shook with the thunderous roar resounding from its heart.

"Where are you?" it boomed.

"Who's that?" croaked Pilgrim muffily.

"Me, of course," boomed the voice, "Professor Balloonafuss".

Heaving and wriggling, the animals squeezed out from under the flabby

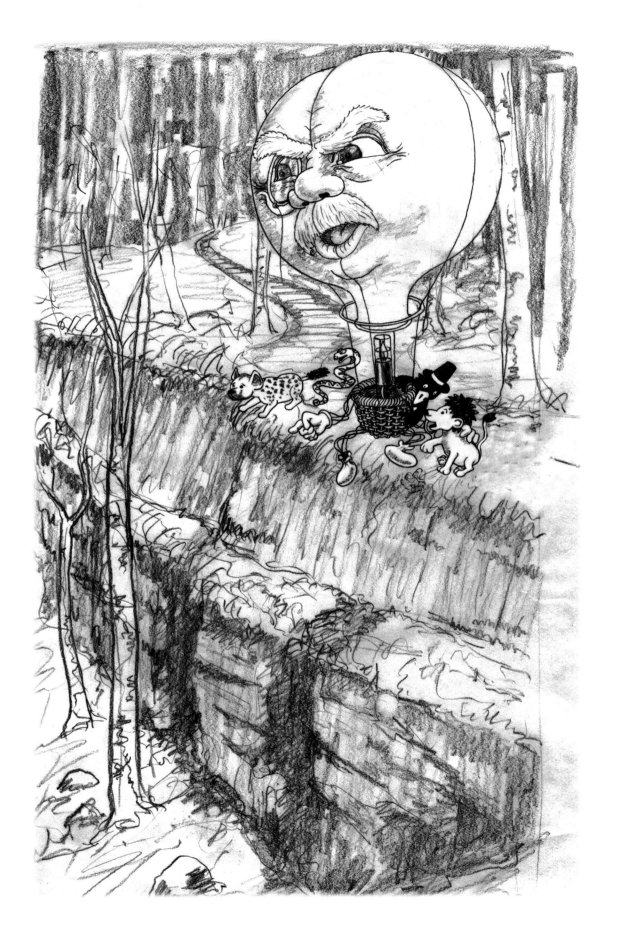

skin of the Professor's huge balloon-head.

"Ha, there you are!" roared the Balloonafuss, as they popped out one by one. "I wondered where you'd got to."

The Animals felt themselves all over to make sure they were all there. Blinking, they looked about them into the night. The stars had retreated to their usual haunts, but seemed dimmer somehow. There was no sign of the flitting flashing lights among the birches, which now shone eerily in the Professor's brilliance.

"What about me!" cried Curd, "I'm down here, look!"

"Wow! Look at dat, would you now?" said Sweeney the Heenie, "a blinking great big hole in de ground. Just where we was about to go."

"And dere's Curd, on dat ledge, dere," said O'Flattery, peering over Sweeney's shoulder.

"It's lucky you cried out, Curdy, or we might've had a nasty accident," added O'Flattery.

A few feet down, clinging on to a narrow grassy ledge, Curd growled: "I did."

Professor Balloonafuss stretched a glove down, "Grab hold of my hand, old boy. That's the ticket. Heave-ho!"

With a tug Curd was jerked into the air and landed, plop, onto the Fuss's forehead, and slid down his silky skin, landing with a thud next to Pilgrim.

They all looked down into the abyss that Mumbie's lamp would have led them into.

"But surely Queen Mumbie-Bumbee wouldn't trick us like that, would she?" asked Curd the Lion.

"Mumbie wouldn't. Of course she wouldn't," said the Balloonafuss, "But those nasty Will-o-the-Wisps would! They love to lure unwitting travellers to their doom. Mumbie's lantern was just a trick of the light to lure you over the cliff. As soon as I saw them looming about you," chuckled the great balloon, "I threaded my way here. They can't stand my brilliance so they fled, unfortunately for young Curd, before I could reach you."

"But how could they do it, turning lights on and off with no electricity?" asked Curd.

"Elementary, my dear Whatnot," said the Balloonafuss, "I'm not Professor of Chimaeristry for nothing, you know."

"What's that?" said Curd.

"Chimaeristry, my dear," he explained, "is the study of things as they seem: as they appear to be. I am master of Chimaeristry, Emphatics and, indeed, of all the Nuisances."

"Talking of nuisances," interrupted Curd, "those Will-o-the-wisps seem to have gone. Have they gone for good?

"I unravelled them so they will never return in that form again, for better or worse. Chimaeristry is the great Nuisance of form-changing, don't you know, from this to that."

"Right enough, it is," agreed Curd, "but I wish things would stay as they were."

"One wouldn't get anywhere if that was the case, dear boy, as I told you last time we met," he said, taking Curd's paw in his weighty fist, "and talking of getting anywhere: it's time we went."

As they marched along, the Professor turned to Sweeney, holding his other glove, and asked: "What's your name, old boy?"

"Heenie," replied Sweeney.

"His knee," retorted the Professor. "His knee. Not He knee. You don't know your grammar."

"No, I never knew me Gran'ma," replied Sweeney, wondering how the Professor could possibly know that. "But she was de backbone of de nation, so de Da t'ought."

"Your Da taught well, old chap. Grammar is the backbone of the nation. It's just a pity you didn't learn it," replied the Balloonafuss. "Damn peculiar name for a fellow - 'His Knee' - all the same."

Sweeney was so befuddled by this that he said not another word.

The Animals joined hands with the unfathomable old Balloonafuss and they danced by the light of the silvery moon until he turned to them and exclaimed: "Oh my, oh my! It's way past my Moon-rise. I'll have to leave you now. Just follow the signs to Nowhere and that is where you'll find Queen Mumbie's house. I'm sure she'll look after you."

As he launched into the air, he added, "She's always prepared to help a good cause."

"Why?" asked O'Flattery.

"Bee-cause!" chuckled the Balloonafuss mysteriously as he rose majestically into the blackboard of the night sky to resume his place among his little pupils, the stars.

CHAPTER TEN.   **The Sign Post.**

Beyond a bend in the track the path divided. Beside the junction stood a signpost. The post was old, worn and lichen-laden and the lettering on its three arms was only just readable.

As the Animals discussed the whys and wheretos of this strange old signpost, they were interrupted by a dark mysterious sigh.

"What was dat?" squeaked O'Flattery, clinging tightly to Sweeney to reassure him that he was there for him, in case things got dangerous.

"Leggo, you fool, you're choking me" spluttered Sweeney.

A second darker sigh washed over them, drowning O'Flattery's apology.

More sighs succeeded one another as waves upon a shingle shore, and the air around them seemed to grow colder with each sigh.

"Perhaps its just the wind?" shuddered Curd.

"Never mind that!" exclaimed Pilgrim, "the point is, which way do we go?"

The Animals looked at one another nervously.

"The one pointing the way we've just come says 'Back Again'," said Curd.

"'Back Again' is no good, is it now?" said O'Flattery, "so what does dat leave?"

"Well, the arm to the right reads 'something, something...WHERE'." said Pilgrim, "I can't read the first bit. And the other arm, pointing straight ahead, says 'Back of Beyond'".

"See dat, Sweeney, me boy," whispered O'Flattery the Snake into

Sweeney's ear, "'Back of Beyond': isn't dat where de Old Corbie Raven lives, accordin' to our man Cranny."

"So 'tis," whispered Sweeney the Heenie, "but we got to get dat Cup from Queen Mumbie first, so we have."

"'Back of Beyond': that sounds an awfully long way," grumbled Curd from the depths of his tummy, "for the time of day, I mean."

"The question is," asked Pilgrim, "What does it mean?"

"IT!" growled a deep voice, "IT?"

"What was THAT?" chorused four voices.

"THAT was my voice," replied the voice, "and I'm not an IT!"

"It come from de post," cried O'Flattery, "dat voice come from de post."

"It couldna," retorted Sweeney, "it's only an auld piece a wood."

"And what do you know, you spotty thing?" cracked the Old Post, "you're only a Toy."

"Wood can't talk," insisted Sweeney, peering around the Post to find the voice.

"If it can talk," suggested Pilgrim, ignoring the argument, "perhaps it will be kind enough to tell us the way to Queen Mumbie's house."

"The way to this, the way to that." grumbled the Post, "That's all folk ever want of me. They ask me way too often for my liking."

"But you're a Signpost, aren't you?" asked Pilgrim, addressing the Post directly for the first time, "You're supposed to know."

"I'm supposed to know," the Post sighed again, "I suppose I do, I suppose I do. But I'm tired of it, don't you see? It wears you down, this endless want, want, want? Nobody cares, you see, nobody ever asks, 'How are you in yourself, Mr Post?' Nobody notices me at all; it's only where I point that matters to them."

Sweeney suddenly asked: "But that's what you're there for, isn't it?"

The Post stood silent for a moment, then from it issued a deep, deep sigh which slowly transformed itself into a guttural groan as one of its old arms subsided until, with a resounding crack, it snapped off and fell to the ground in a cloud of dust and powdery splinters. The Animals looked at Sweeney.

"I didn't say nuttin," said Sweeney, going a little pink.

"Years, it's taken; years and years of neglect and ignorance," said the Post, ignoring Sweeney, "not a 'By-your-leave', not a 'Thank-you', not ever!" he creaked, as another arm drooped sadly.

"No, no, please..." said Curd

"What's the point in going on?"

"...Don't lose another arm." said Sweeney.

"I can't bear it any more," sighed the Post.

"WE care!" shouted Pilgrim, surprising himself, "honest, we do."

"Well, if you really mean it," grumbled the Post.

"Yes, yes! T'ink of all dem people who'll be glad of you pointing de way to where dey're going," said Sweeney the Heenie.

"That's just it, don't you see? Where THEY'RE going." the Post creaked, "I'm going nowhere!"

"But so are we!" cried Curd.

"What?"

"Don't you see?" explained Curd, "Nowhere is where we're all going!"

The Old Post just groaned louder, so Curd quickly added: "because Nowhere is where Queen Mumbie-Bumbee lives, and we're going there now."

"To tell her how important you are," Pilgrim added quickly.

"And den she'll come with all her carpenters and painters and fix you up again like new," added Sweeney.

"That would be nice," sighed the Old Sign Post, "some new arms would be nice."

"Some new directions, too," suggested Pilgrim, "perhaps a little simpler?"

"Wid brand new letters," said Sweeney loudly.

"All in gold paint," said O'Flattery, louder.

"Well, if you're going Nowhere - it's that-a-way!" said the Post.

"Which away?" asked Curd, "I can't tell which way you're pointing."

"I'm not pointing nowhere," answered the enigmatic Old Stick.

"Eh?"

"Look, Nowhere is the way I'm NOT pointing."

"Oh, he means de missing arm," explained Sweeney, "Is that right?"

"Mmm, I suppose," muttered the Post, knowing his new companions would desert him now. "Remember me to Queen Mumbie, wherever she is."

"We will, we will," shouted the Animals as they scampered off along the path to Nowhere.

CHAPTER ELEVEN.   Mumbie's Hospitality.

Soon they arrived at a little door set in the hollow under the roots of a gnarled and ancient hawthorn tree. Set beside the little door was a brass bell-pull, which Pilgrim Crow tugged firmly.

A low hum began to throb around them as if the little door was wondering whether to let them enter or not. Then a strange device above the door began to glow with a warm golden light, pulsing in time with the hum of the bell.

"It looks like a bee," said Sweeney, as the animals looked up, "and dem stripes looks more and more alphabetical," he added.

"Why, so they do," said Pilgrim the Learned Cleric, "N...O..."

"What's it say?" asked Curd.

"NOWHERE." read Pilgrim.

"Ah, so THIS is it," said Curd the Lion. "I always wondered where No-where was. This is where everything goes that gets lost, you know."

"Why?" asked Sweeney the Heenie.

"'Cos, when something gets lost, people say it's Nowhere to be found. So maybe our lost Brooch is here," said Curd brightly. "There must be all sorts of treasures here."

"To be sure," agreed O'Flattery, nudging Sweeney knowingly, thinking of the cracked Cup they had to steal from Queen Mumbie-Bumbee for Mother Beanie, Old Corbie's washer-woman.

Pilgrim tugged on the bell-pull. They heard a distant jingle from within and, after a short pause, the little door swung ajar, and golden light shone

upon the assembled animals.

"Good evening," hummed a soft voice out of the centre of the light.
Blinking in the brightness, they began slowly to make out the stripy form

71

of a furry friendly-looking bee, standing in a narrow hallway, wearing a large pink hat with a little veil, rubbing its little hands together fussily, as it politely awaited their reply.

"Thank you," replied Pilgrim, bowing, "and are you... well... her Majesty Queen Mumbie-Bumbee?"

"I am indeed, and very well, thank you for asking," said the Queen. "But do call me 'Mumbie'," she added, as the animals filed through the door into the hall.

"Excuse me, Ma'am," said Pilgrim.

"Mumbie, please," the Queen interrupted gently.

"Mumbie," continued Pilgrim, "about that sign above the door?"

"You noticed it?" smiled Mumbie, "That is the most important lesson a bee can learn. By that a bee learns her exact place in the world."

"How is dat, Mumbie?" asked Sweeney, beemused.

"Why, beeing Now-here, one can bee No-where else," she hummed beenignly as she shut the front door, "and that is a lesson all subjects must understand."

"All what subjects?" asked Sweeney, looking around. The hall was empty save for themselves and the Queen.

"All **my** subjects..."

"Your subjects?" repeated Sweeney, "but where are your subjects?"

"Fetching..." she replied.

"What are they fetching?" asked Curd, hoping it might be some honey.

"What are they fetching?" repeated the Queen haughtily, "why, nothing, of course."

"But how can they be fetching, if they are not bringing anything?" asked Pilgrim, his curiosity aroused.

"Because they are beecoming," replied the Queen triumphantly waving her several arms as if in greeting to her approaching subjects.

The animals looked quickly towards the door, which remained firmly shut, then at each other, and shrugged their shoulders, thinking Mumbie must be slightly batty.

"Very beecoming, yes indeed," purred the Queen to her herself. She turned to the little band, "but you must be cold, tired and hungry. Come into my chamber and have a bite."

"This is what I call hospitality," chuckled Sweeney, "I'm dying for a bite."

O'Flattery tensed with fright. "Great-grandfather died in hospitality from a bee-bite!" he hissed as Sweeney choked.

"Hospital, stupid," croaked Pilgrim, "not hospitality; and bees sting, not bite. Now be quiet."

"He was stunk, den, by a bee," grumbled O'Flattery, "and died of an allergic."

The Animals stepped through a circular door into her chamber. Dimly lit by the lamp in the hall, Queen Mumbie's chamber was a small round room with a bare hard-packed earthen floor. Its walls and ceiling were beamed with the roots of the tree beneath which she lived. Not far from the door a fireplace was set into the wall. It was laid with birch bark tinder and logs, but had not been lit.

Wondering why not, since the weather was bitterly cold, Curd asked.

"You know, I can't quite remember why," mumbled the Queen, " I keep meaning to light it, but seem to fall asleep before getting around to it." She yawned. "But let's do it now."

She lit a taper of bark and thrust it into the centre of the heap, fanning the first flickering flames with whirring wings. The whirring soon grew to a roar as the logs began to blaze cheerfully, casting a golden glow through the chamber. The animals gathered round to share the warmth.

As they grew accustomed to the light, they ventured to look more carefully around the room.

In its centre was a magnificent six-poster bed, its pillars carved with intertwining bee-chains, climbing up to a canopy depicting a wonderful beehive scene. Here were the Queen and all her subjects, thousands of bees, busy about their business in a land of honeyed marquetry.

In the centre of the bed itself a pillow lay decorated with beautiful embroidery depicting many more subjects. Subjects of all sorts: flowers, trees, birds, animals and bees, wonderfully intermingled to suggest all manner of stories.

Beyond the bed, quite close to the fireplace, there was, set in the wall, two inviting little yellow doors shaped like the old-fashioned bee-hives on a honey-pot, with shiny brass latches, stared at them like a pair of bright eyes.

Below the little doors, on a neat little shelf, stood an old cracked cup and a spoon so bent that the head of the handle met the base of the spoon.

O'Flattery nudged Sweeney: the old cracked Cup!

Above the doors hung a stern warning notice: BEE-WARE!

"Oh dear," thought O'Flattery, "she must have it guarded."

"You know, Queen Mumbie-Bumbee..." began Curd.

"Your Majesty," interrupted Sweeney, "we're looking for Old Corbie, de Raven, and we were directed to come to you by Nook and Cranny..."

"Oh, the mine goblins? How are they?" said Queen Mumbie. "Such a long time since they've been round. Not since the fall," said the Queen, "not since they came for their annual honey-fest."

73

The Queen caught sight of Sweeney and O'Flattery staring hard at her cupboard, and asked "Pardon me for asking, but you are not a Bear, by any chance?" Her voice trembled querulously as she hopped from one foot to another, performing a nervous quadrille around the room. "You see, I'm not fond of Bears. They come snatching our honey without so much as a please or thank you."

"No, not at all, at all," said Sweeney, "I'm a Heenie."

"Do Heenies like honey?" she asked nervously.

"Heenies love honey," Sweeney laughed.

The Queen looked anxiously away in all directions.

"…but we always ask first," Sweeney added.

"Oh, my goodness," sighed Queen Mumbie, not quite sure whether Heenies asked first, then snatched, or the other way round.

By and by she calmed down and opened the left-hand door onto the most beautiful sight! A golden honeycomb, dripping with honey, filled the entire cupboard. "Just pull the table over here, will you, dears?" said the Queen, scooping spoonfuls of the honey into a small bowl, "and get some glasses and plates and sit yourselves down."

Mumbie then went into the other cupboard and lifted out a pile of cakes and mince-pies. "These cakes," she explained as she placed the tray before them, "are honey-cakes. Made to a special recipe, handed down from Queen to Queen. They are a mixture of nuts, honey and secret spices, heaped into a little hive, and baked till they reached a rich golden brown."

"Yummy," said Sweeney, rubbing his round belly, "my favourite."

"Do have one," she said as she offered each in turn, adding, "a dab of honey, dear?" as she spooned honey onto each cake, regardless.

"The mince-pies I buy in from those awful Magpies," she said with a shudder.

With much lip smacking and crunching the animals dug sizeable quarries into the honey-cake hills and mince-pie mountains. Queen Mumbie returned with a tray on which stood four little glasses and a golden flagon.

"A drink, dears?" She poured some golden liquid into the cups. "This is Mumbie's finest home-brewed Mumble-mead."

"Very more-ish, dis mead," said Sweeney, holding his cup out for a third time.

"Talking of Moors," said Mumbie-Bumbee, pouring more of the amber nectar, "You mentioned you are looking for Old Corbie the Great Raven."

"You know him?" asked Pilgrim Crow, reluctantly sipping from his first cup.

"Oh, yes," she replied, "Old Corbie and I go back a long way. We used to be friends you know. But we had a disagreement. But why are looking for him?"

"Well, he stole Mother's precious brooch, you see," began Pilgrim, "but Henry and Henrietta got the blame and we're all going to sold off unless Mother gets her brooch back by their Birthday – they're twins, you see – and there's only two days left so you see we're in a hurry…"

"Dear me! You do talk such a lot all at once," interrupted Queen Mumbie, "one gets quite breathless. Well, if Old Corbie the Raven has STOLEN Mother's brooch, I will certainly try to show you the way."

"See, see?" hissed O'Flattery to Sweeney.

"My memory is not what it was," Mumbie continued, "but Old Corbie lives somewhere up on the rocks of the moorland up yonder. I'll show you in the morning how to get there. But now - your health!"

By the time they had drunk their health several times, to please the Queen, and were no longer sure which was who's, the evening had slipped dreamily into night.

"Scuse me, Queen Mumbie," Curd suddenly asked, "but when will all your subjects be coming? Isn't it getting a bit late?"

He had been quietly awaiting their arrival all evening.

"They are beecoming as we are beecoming," replied the Queen helpfully.

"Oh?" muttered Curd feeling more beewildered than beecoming.

While the Queen was distracted, O'Flattery seized his chance and her cracked cup and hid it in his coils as she bumbled on. He felt very pleased with his sneaky theft because he knew that she had stolen it from Old

Corbie in the first place. So he was just going to RETURN it to its rightful owner, which was a good thing to do. Wasn't it?

"Now that you have eaten," she said, "what about a little beemusement?"

"What's that taste like," asked Curd, feeling very full.

"I think she means 'amusement'", said Pilgrim loudly, "it means fun and ga…"

"I mean bee-musement," retorted the Queen, who had overheard, "ordinary mortals amuse themselves; we bees beemuse ourselves. Shall we begin?"

"Er, yes, why not," said Pilgrim, first among them to gather his wits. "Let's start with a little song, then, to warm ourselves up." And so she began:

"Fastnagumbo, fastnagumbo,"
Mumbo-jumbo sadly cried:
"Fastnagumbo, fastnagumbo;
Me laces is untied."

"How do I bumblo widout Gumbo
Through da Mumbo-jumbo mud?
In deeply junglo, how I cumbo
Through da Mumbo-jumbo flood?"

By and by there flew Balooba;
A great Balooba bird it flied.
With a Tuba, all bran-newba,
Its newba Tuba trade it plied.

Through and through its newba Tuba
A bubbly Tuba-tune it blew;
Loud it blew: "Hullabalooba,"
Loudly blew, "hullabaloo!"

High the great Balooba flewba,
Over the mushy marshes wide;
Till it heard that sad "Yoo-hooba!"
And there the Mumbo-jumbo spied.
Soft it landed, feet expanded,

On the squishy-squashy mud;
Balooba-walked and Tuba-talked
Through the plishy-ploshy flood.

"Fastnagumbo, fastnagumbo,"
Mumbo-jumbo trumpeted;
"Glad you cumbo do me gumbo,
Me laces is undid."

Jumbo pointed to his gumbo,
Showed him how they should be thread.
Now knew Balooba what to dooba:
To tie the laces bent his head.

Hard he stared at Jumbo's gumbo;
Hard, hard he stared those gumbos through.
But where the laces, Dumbo-jumbo,
Should be thread, just dark holes grew.
So he left that Elephantic

Mumbie's Hospitality

Crying in its plight so frantic;
Flew across the broad Atlantic,
To those places, so romantic,
Sailors sing of them in song.

There he found sought-after traces
In Sargasso, in the places
Where, between the ocean races,
Sleek and long, like lovely laces,
Sargasso eels swam, bright and strong.

He caught two eels, sleek and strong,
Despite their squeals, loud and long,
Despite their antic, flew along,
Without a word, without a song,
Flew to Afric', right or wrong,
With Mumbo-jumbo's brand-new thong.

He thread the eels in Jumbo's gumbo,
He laced them up and tied them good.
Into the mud jumped Mumbo-jumbo,
Splashing happy as he could.

Once in the oozy mud of Mumbo,
Once in the Mumbo-jumbo flood,
Those sleek and slippery eels from gumbo
Slid into the slimy mud.

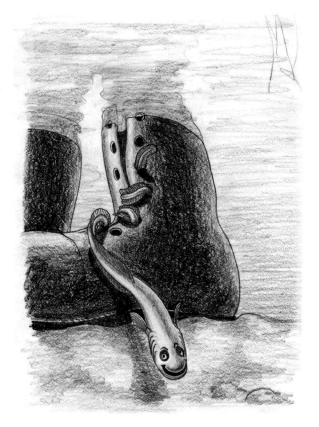

Sargasso grins upon their faces,
They upped and vanished without traces
Into the wet and boggy places,
Onto the soft and soggy places,
Of the Mumbo-jumbo bog.

Jumbo was, still wondering why,
Sucked down by soggy soles to lie
In places where the flatfish fly;
His last goodbye, a deep sad sigh,
Just slowly bubbled from the bog.

Though tied as hard as he could doodba,

Those laces were undid.
Poor Balooba dropped his Tuba,
And flew away and hid."

"I t'ink I got one," shouted Sweeney so loud that O'Flattery nearly dropped the Cup.
"Off you go then dear," said Queen Mumbie-Bumbee.
"It's called 'De Grateful Mouse' and it goes like dis," began Sweeney.

"Hey, diddle, diddle,
De Rat wid a riddle
Was grating cheese from de Moon;
De little Mouse laughed
To see it ground down,
As he scooped it all up wid a spoon."

"Sounds strangely familiar, somehow," said the Queen, "but jolly good anyway."
"It's fiddle-de-dee, if you ask me," said Pilgrim cattily.
"Right-oh. Now for a round of bee-musements," said the Queen, rubbing her little hands together, "Whose going to go first?"
"I don't need to," said Curd the Lion, "I haven't finished my drink yet."
The Queen looked quizzically at him, and since no one else spoke, she said: "Ahem. Well, *Why is pointing out a bee like learning the alphabet?*"
No one spoke again.
"Because you say: '*There's a bee, see?*" said Mumbie-Bumbee, answering her own question, "A, B, C... Get it?"
"Ah." Pilgrim in his bemusement spoke for them all.
"Here's another. This should be right up your street," said the Queen, "*Why is a Raven taking a Jewel like Ink drawn from a Well?*"
The Animals all looked at each other.
"Right-ho," said Queen Mumbie, "We'll take it in turns. Now you try first, Curd."
"I've tried, but I'm tired," said Curd, "of thinking: it's this ink thing..."
"I've got one!" shouted Sweeney, jumping up and down, "*Because each needs a quill.*"
"Bravo! Nearly well done," said the Queen. Then seeing Curd's dismay, she added, "here's an answer for you: *Because both are associated with acquire (a quire).*"
"But neither can sing," protested Curd.
"Oh, dear," said Queen Mumbie-Bumbee, "try this for an answer, then:

Because each requires righting (writing) immediately."

There was not a word from the Animals, neither cheer nor clap.

"Well I never," she said, looking a little disconcerted, "what about this then? *Because black beginnings end well in both.*"

"Zzzzzzzzzz…"

All the animals had fallen asleep where they sat, except Sweeney, who mumbled drowsily as Queen Mumbie put them all to bed, "so dat's what it means to be horribly bored by a bee." He heaved himself onto Mumbie's bed and laid his head on her beautifully embroidered feather pillow.

In a few moments he was in the Land of Nod (but that's another story…)

CHAPTER TWELVE.   **Through Dawley Wood.**

Peeping out of Mumbie's front door, the four bleary-eyed Adventurers looked at each other and shivered.

The ground was covered in a layer of snow. Curd's 'blanket of cloud' had fallen literally to wrap the entire landscape in its white down. Suddenly his wish of the night before under the icy stars seemed no longer so warm and comforting.

They paused. Before them, their breath steamed in the freezing air; behind, their backs toasted in the hot air gusting out from Mumbie's chamber.

"Come along. We'd better get moving through the wood," said Mumbie. "You've a field to cross before you reach the shelter of Dawley Wood. You don't want to be caught napping in the open when the Rooks and Jackdaws come looking for you, do you?"

The animals, with Queen Mumbie buzzing around them fussily, marched along the boulder-strewn hillside of the northern part of Birkwood, which is what Mumbie called this part of the wood.

Curd kept a sharp eye out in case any wandering Birks appeared. "Are Birks dangerous, Queen Mumbie?" he asked.

"Birks? Of course not," she replied, "they're all around you."

"Where? I can't see any?" Curd looked around nervously, wondering if Birks were experts at hiding themselves, because he couldn't see a single one.

"Birk is the old name the Birch tree, and they're all around, as you can

see," she laughed.

Gradually the birch trees thinned out before them and here, where the wind-driven snow had not covered them, the rocks were soft with a greeny-blue down of lichen and moss. The ground on either side of the path grew a stubble of bilberry and bracken, hoary in the morning frost.

Reaching the wall that bounded her Queendom, Mumbie alighted upon it. Pointing east as the others climbed up to join her, she said: "That's where you must go. That's Hollywood." She pointed to a dense wood of holly-trees which lay like a white ghostly long-barrow beyond the open fields.

"Holywood," corrected Pilgrim Crow, who knew about such things.

"As you like," agreed the Queen, "but my advice is this: don't travel East directly. You are sure to be spotted in the open. Go north across that little field to the copse by Dawley Farm. Then go east, skirting the farm, following the copses round in a circle southward till you reach Hollywood itself. I must leave you now; this cold makes me so sleepy."

The cawing of the first rooks and jackdaws straggling across the sky from their roosts heralded the start of the hunt.

"Watch out, now; especially for the daws on the farm chimneys," warned Mumbie as she warmed her wings to return to her home.

"Doors? I don't see any doors on the chimneys." said Curd.

"Daws, stupid! Jackdaws. They must perch up there on lookout," snapped Pilgrim. "Follow in each others' footsteps," he added, "then they'll think there's only one of us."

"Which one?" Curd asked, "I hope it isn't me."

As they set off, O'Flattery tugged Sweeney back: "Psst! Look what I got."

"Heh, you little Divil," chuckled Sweeney, seeing the cracked cup hidden in O'Flattery's colourful coils.

The Animals looked longingly back at the diminishing stripy back of Queen Mumbie-Bumbee, meandering down the path to her home.

Emerging from the lee of the cold grey stone wall into the icy draught of the north wind, the warm glow of Mumbie's hospitality seemed to recede with her into a twilit world of long ago and far away.

In their long hesitation, each saw in the others' eyes the notion of abandoning their Great Adventure for a return to that cosy haven.

"Look!" cried Curd. "Look at the sky!"

The sky was skeined with crooked threads of rooks and jackdaws fanning out from their night-roosts. Two of these threads were heading in their direction!

The animals dashed across the vast expanse of the little meadow towards a stone stile set in the wall opposite the farm. On its far side stood a large holly-tree, its deep leaf-green hollow beckoning shelter as it leaned over the wall like a ragged frost-giant.

They scrambled onto the stile as the first of the birds arrived overhead, and dived into the prickly shelter of the dense holly-tree just as a piercing scream announced they had been seen. A jackdaw swooped down and landed on the stile, to be joined by another, chattering loudly.

"I spotted one, Dora," said the first bird, "one of them Nanimals we were told to watch out fer."

"You sure, Jack, dear," said the second. "I didn't see nuffink!"

"You disbelievin' me, Dora? I saw a yellow fing streakin' across into this here bush, I tell yer."

A host of noisy birds gathered along the wall, perched in the upper branches of the holly-tree, and strutted arrogantly in the thick snow. The tree was surrounded.

Sweeney, who was uncomfortably pinned between two prickling branches, backed further into the undergrowth and, finding there a nice soft patch, sat on it. A muffled squeal and sharp nip on his rump made him jump, and a yellow-brown flash shot from under his feet, out from under the tree, and away across the snow. It was a weasel!

A tremendous chattering and fluttering was followed by the departure of all but the first two jackdaws.

"Come on Jack, it was ony a Weasel," said Dora, "an its gone now, innit?"

"No it ain't. It were a Nanimal like I toldja," insisted Jack. "It 'ad spots an its still 'ere."

"Perhaps it was a measley weasel, an' you wouldn't want to catch that! But there's no tellin' you, is there, Jack, lad," scolded Dora before flying to the nearby chimney stack.

The Jack-jackdaw flew to the ground and strutted angrily through the snow around the tree, peering into the darkness behind the dense curtain of snow, searching for the measley weasel that wasn't, but not daring to come in lest the not-measley weasel proved to be a stoatally more dangerous creature "I see'd, I know I did," he insisted.

At this distance they could clearly see his bright eye standing out like pearl against the sooty mask of his face and his ashen grey collar.

After a few minutes the jackdaw gave up and returned to the farm chimney with his mate.

"Phew!" Curd sighed, "At last we can go."

"Keep out of sight of the farm," warned Pilgrim.

Dashing from holly-tree to holly-tree, they made their way in fits and starts through the copses on the northern side of the farm, keeping at all times a holly-tree between themselves and the jackdaws on the farm roof.

They at last reached the southern edge of Dawley Wood. Across a short rock-strewn pasture the densely-packed snow-covered trees of Holywood lay like a low hill pocked with dark tunnels. Suddenly a raucous commotion made them stop. Pilgrim flew to the top of the nearest holly-tree to spy out from its shelter.

"What is it?" shouted Curd in a hoarse whisper.

"There's a flurry of rooks mobbing something white. It's a bird... two... no three... seagulls, I think."

"Bullies!" shouted Curd who, forgetting himself in his anger, found himself charging across the field to the rescue of the stricken gulls.

A moment later Pilgrim flew into the fray, and the pair sent feathers flying as they fought, attracting a host of mobbing rooks onto themselves in turn.

Jackdaws had by now joined the mobbing rooks, and Curd and Pilgrim disappeared under a dark cloud of feathers. This was too much for Sweeney. He charged towards the thickest knot of birds, uttering a blood-curdling cackle of laughter with a flabbergasted O'Flattery clinging speechlessly to his neck.

The unearthly cackling of this strange spotted and striped two-headed beast charging towards them startled the rooks and jackdaws into flight, freeing Curd, Pilgrim and the seagulls to run for the sanctuary of Holywood.

Safe in the margins of Holywood, they watched the confused rooks wheeling and diving, squabbling about whose fault it was they had lost their quarry.

"Forever in your debt," said the first gull, bowing low towards Sweeney and Curd, who was the first to charge.

"T'was nuttin' at all," said Sweeney, casually waving aside his thanks. Curd modestly said nothing.

"Let us introduce ourselves," said the gull to Sweeney. "Pathos, myself. Ethos and Erymos, my companions-in-arms, at your service, Sir."

"And I'm Sweeney de Heenie, champion of de plain man, at yours," boasted Sweeney.

Soon Sweeney and the three gulls were getting along famously, exchanging jokes and cackling loudly, until Pilgrim cut them short with a sharp croak: "When you four have quite finished, we had better decide what to do before those Rooks come looking for us."

"May we suggest a diversion?" suggested Pathos.

"We've no time for games," snapped Pilgrim.

"We'll distract them," said Ethos, "while you make your escape."

"Don't be silly, you'll be caught again," said Pilgrim.

"No we won't. We were ambushed. We're ready this time, and we are much faster than they are," answered Erymos.

With that, the three gulls were off, rocketing away over the heads of the surprised rooks, which quickly flew in pursuit.

"We'd better go deeper into the woods," said Pilgrim, "before they come after us."

The Animals walked deeper into the darkness of the wood.

"Did you hear what our friends, de gulls, said?" said Sweeney suddenly, egged on by O'Flattery's whispers, "Dey said that if ever I needed deyr help, dey wouldn't refuse. Who won't dey refuse, Pilgrim? Not you, Curd; nor you, Pilgrim. Me. And why did dey say that? Because I saved dem. I, wid me blood-curdling cry. And who was it fought off de Rats, single-handed. I did. And who escaped de Magpies? I, Sweeney the Heenie."

"What are you gibbering about?" asked Pilgrim.

"What I'm talking about is dis. Why should Curd de Lion be leader of dis Crusade? Just because of his name? He's done nothing brave nor clever neither. He's been caught by magpies, swept into de river by de Hag, and nearly smothered by rooks and jackdaws. Dat's what I'm talking about, now. Some Leader, indeed!"

"And what do you propose?" sneered Pilgrim.

"Dat if you wants a leader, I'm your only man," said Sweeney.

"Ah," said Pilgrim, "is this mutiny? Is this Rebellion?"

"It's Justice!" said Sweeney. "Justice for de plain man. I didn't have any say when Curd was made Leader, now, did I? You, de cleric, decided. So now I've decided. I've decided I'm going to be de Leader from now on."

"Hmm," Pilgrim thought for a moment. "I'll tell you what. We'll have a contest. We'll split into two groups, and the one to lead his group first to the other end of the wood will be declared Leader of the Adventure. That's just, isn't it?"

"Piece-a-cake," said Sweeney, "I'll take O'Flattery, here; and you, Curd, take Pilgrim."

O'Flattery whispered slyly, "Don't worry, Sweeney, me lad, Curd couldna find his way out of a paper bag."

While they had been talking they had wandered far into the twilight world of the wood. Pale-barked pillars of holly arched overhead to support the dark vaulted roof of leaves. Boulders lay in the deep leaf-litter like fallen masonry, giving the whole wood the ruinous air of a crumbling crypt. There was no snow on the ground here. They stopped at a place where the path appeared to fork into two, both branches leading obliquely southward.

"Which way?" asked Curd, politely.

"I'll take de path to de left," said Sweeney, "and you take de path dat's left. Right?"

So saying, he marched off briskly with O'Flattery fluttering about his neck.

"But Sweeney," Curd called after him, "that means I'll be following you."

"And dat," Sweeney shouted back, "is as it should be!"

Then he spoke this verse:
  "Left to right
  Imbalance,
  Time might;
  But is it right
  Left dis way?"
and marched off into the twilight until only his cackling laughter remained.

  "Curd," said Pilgrim, "the one that is left for the other, after one has taken the left, is the right, not the left, right?"
  "No. What do you mean?"
  "We take the right-hand path," croaked Pilgrim in despair, "let's go. We're going this way now, right or wrong."
  "Right or left," corrected Curd gloomily, as the pair stumped deeper and deeper into the wood.

CHAPTER THIRTEEN.   **Guests and Strangers.**

Curd and Pilgrim picked their way carefully between the rocks scattered under the evergreen vaults of Holywood.

"Ouch!" cried Curd, as he stubbed his toe on a small rock protruding from the ground.

"I was thinking," he said, after a pause.

"Don't." said Pilgrim.

"Its dark," said Curd.

"Yes," said Pilgrim, "So what?"

"At least we can't be seen," said Curd.

"No," said Pilgrim, "we can't."

"But..." started Curd.

"But what?" snapped Pilgrim irritably, stopping again.

"Neither can we..." said Curd, and broke off into silence.

"What? Not see?" asked Pilgrim.

"No. I mean yes. We can't see..." said Curd, not quite seeing how to put it, "see if we are being seen, or not, if you see what I mean."

"But if we can't be seen, it doesn't matter if we can't see if we can't be seen, silly," said Pilgrim.

"Oh," said Curd; after a short pause, "if we can't see we can't be seen - then how can we know we can't?"

"We don't!" said Pilgrim.

"I see," said Curd, looking about him, wondering which shadow might be doing the seeing he couldn't see it doing.

They shuffled through leaves, and squelched through mud in silence for a few more minutes, occasionally stubbing a toe upon a rock they had missed in the dark. As they plodded on, their several paws made a peculiar trash-trash-trashing noise in the dead leaf-litter.

"That's strange," said Curd, interrupting the silence yet again.

"What is it this time?" asked Pilgrim, who was doing his best to pretend he knew which way they should be going.

"It's strange how loud everything becomes when you can't see very well," said Curd.

"What do you mean?" said Pilgrim.

"Like that funny trash-trash-trash noise which keeps going along with us," said Curd.

"You're right. It is loud," said Pilgrim.

They paused to listen.

Trash-trash-trash.

"Stop moving," ordered Pilgrim.

"I'm not!" said Curd.

They listened again.

Silence.

They moved off, trash-trash-trash-trash, through the night, or day, or whatever it was, accompanied by the uneasy feeling that all was not as it should be. It seemed to each that the trash-trash-trash didn't match his footsteps, which were distinctly smaller.

This Uneasy Feeling seized each of them by the scruff of the neck with its prickly jaws.

"Stop!" whispered Pilgrim, urgently.

Trash-trash-trash.

Silence.

"Did you hear that?" whispered Pilgrim.

"What - it's stopped," whispered Curd.

"Exactly. But not when we did. We're not alone." said Pilgrim.

They set off again, a little faster.

"It's following us," said Curd.

"What is?" flapped Pilgrim in alarm. "My eyes aren't so good in the dark."

Curd looked.

"It's… it's… a NIGHTBEAR!" cried Curd, "Just like in my dream… a NIGHTBEAR!"

"Rubbish," said Pilgrim, turning round, "It's…"

He stopped.

There, some distance away in the gloom, a huge black shaggy bear-like beast sat upon its haunches; its great head swaying to and fro as if searching for something; its eyes as big as saucers, glowing like live coals in the darkness.

"It's a… giant… DOG!" stammered Pilgrim, aghast. "It's a BAR-GUEST!"

At that moment the great beast's head swung to face them; its great saucer-eyes fiercely staring straight through them, as if it had latched onto the sound of its own name.

"Run!" yelled Pilgrim.

The great dog started forward as they took to their heels, and its heavy trash-trash-trash loped a short distance behind their scurrying feet.

As Curd ran, he began to wonder why it was that the Barguest had stopped when they stopped, and why it only seemed to see them when they moved or made a loud noise. Suddenly he had an idea.

"Stop!" Curd hissed in a whisper, "Not a sound!"

Pilgrim froze in his tracks.

Trash-trash-trash… The great dog ran on a few paces and then stopped.

They looked round. The Barguest was standing some distance behind them, its great head swinging back and forth. Its saucer-eyes glowed as it searched about. It stared directly at them several times, but didn't seem to see them in the dark.

"I'm right," whispered Curd, "It can only find and follow us by the noises we make."

Pilgrim coughed.

The shaggy beast looked at them questioningly, advanced a few paces, and stopped again. It was so close now they could hear its panting breath. Pilgrim looked at Curd, realising now what he meant.

The pair backed away very slowly, cautiously avoiding any dry leaves. Pace by pace they retreated from the Barguest. When they had put a good few yards between themselves and the beast. Curd whispered, "Let's go."

Turning to go, Curd snapped a dry twig with a hollow "crack!"

At this the dog jumped up and ran towards them. Curd ran full-tilt into the first tree he encountered, and rebounded backwards.

The shaggy beast galloped towards them, its heavy paws trashing the ground as it came. Its cavernous jaws gaped wide, great yellow-stained teeth set like a gin-trap. Its lolling tongue flicked pearly chains of saliva droplets about its head as it charged, uttering a weird, unearthly, wailing shriek.

Before they could scream or run, it struck, and was gone, knocking Pilgrim flying and squashing Curd.

But it was gone! Racing on into the gloomy depths of the wood, churning up clods of earth as it went.

They had barely time to realize that they were still alive before an even stranger apparition leaped over them in pursuit of the first, "Tally-HO!"

"What was THAT?"

Curd and Pilgrim slowly picked themselves up, shaken and muddy, and were about to brush it all off as a bad dream when the second apparition returned.

A strange, balding, white-haired and white-armoured Knight came trotting towards them, holding in his left hand a long lance, and riding the strangest of mounts.

"Missed the Beast, but I'll get him next time," said the Knight.

"Excuse me, but are you the White Knight in the book?" said Curd the Lion.

"What book?" asked the Knight.

"Alice through the Looking Glass," replied Pilgrim.

"Stuff and nonsense! If I WAS in a book, I would be a mere Page, not a Knight. Do I look at all flat to you? No." said the Knight, answering his own question, "and here's another thing: just how big is this book?"

"About eight inches tall, I guess," said Pilgrim, "at least, the Twin's is."

"Well, there you are then! I could comfortably fit a book that size into my saddle-bag. And if I did that, why, I would find myself in my own saddle-bag, and then where would I be? No, my little fellows, I am Sir Rush, noble Knight of Babylon," announced the Knight grandly, "and this is my Kalandar."

His Kalandar was a curious beast. It had the head, tail, and scales of a serpent, the front legs of a lion, the hind-legs and claws of an eagle, with possibly a few other creatures thrown in for good measure.

"He doesn't look much like a horse," said Curd to Pilgrim, "I thought

Knights rode horses."

"Only in books," replied the Knight. "Here we ride what we like, don't we, dear?"

"I thought you said he was a Calender?" asked Curd. "I thought a calendar was for keeping up to date with."

"So he is, aren't you, Kalandar, dear?" said the Knight, patting its long neck. "He's a Beast for All Seasons."

Curd and Pilgrim stood side-by-side in respectful silence as the Knight leaped down from his mount and stood before them.

Bowing graciously, the good Knight introduced himself: "Sir Rufus Albinus Nigel Rush, Knight, at your service, dear chaps."

The Animals looked at one another, wondering what to say. With a string of names like that, where does one begin?

"Ah," said Sir Rush, guessing their dilemma, "but call me Sir Rufus for short".

Pilgrim, who had Education, realised that all these names were colours, and asked, "Why do call yourself Sir Rufus when your hair is so white? Surely Rufus would suit someone with red hair, and yours is so…"

"White? Oh, of course it's Albinus, now. Rufus is so yesterday! Why didn't you remind me, Kalandar, dear? It's my hair, you see," explained the Knight, "once red as flame, now as white as snow, it will be become black as a mystery soon."

Pilgrim stood there, beak agape, at a loss for words.

How could he bring himself to tell this poor knight that he was simply losing his hair, and not growing, as he seemed to think, a fine new crop of black hair? How could he break the news to this brave knight, who had just rescued them from that terrible beast, the Barguest, that he was simply going BALD?

"You haven't yet asked me why I am growing my hair black next," said Sir Rush, quite unperturbed. "Why, the better to catch the Barguest, of course! I am having a suit of black armour made especially! 'Ye Blakke Knyghte of Brimastane' I will be," he said dreamily, with a large sweep of his hand through the air, as if across a sign, "depicted in letters of pure gold."

He turned sharply on them, making them twitch. "Enough of that! I haven't time to babble on; I'm in a rush, you know."

Sir Rush walked a few paces away from them, raised his lance to his shoulder with both hands, rushed towards his charger at a furious pace, vaulted right over its back, and disappeared over the other side.

Curd and Pilgrim crept cautiously round the Kalandar. Keeping well away from its serpent-head, they found Sir Rush sitting on the ground, his

feet splayed out in front of him.

"Tremendous!" Sir Rush roared with laughter. "My greatest leap to-date! If only the blessed Kalandar had not moved."

"But it didn't move," Curd pointed out.

"It did move. It definitely moved. From where I was, there IT was, getting

closer all the time, until suddenly it dived under me. Still, no point in arguing over what's past and done with, eh?"

"No, no, of course not," agreed Curd, helping the Knight to his feet.
Sir Rush obviously had his own peculiar way of looking at the world, and
they would need his help to find Sweeney and O'Flattery in this dreadful
wood, and their own way out of it.

"Sir Albinus," began Curd.

"Sir Rush, dear creature," corrected the Knight jovially, "let's dispense
with formalities like first-names. Call me by my surname, Sir Rush. After
all, we're almost friends."

"Sir Name," said Curd, "I, I mean, Sir Rush. We are lost and hungry…"

"Are you, indeed?" Sir Rush looked surprised and amused. "And which
of you is Lost?"

"We both are," said Curd.

"Hmmm," nodded the Knight, "And need I ask which is Hungry?"

"We both are," said Curd,.

"Well, how is a fellow to tell you apart? Where I come from, we name
what we see, as we see what we name," said the peculiar old Knight.

"Why?" asked Curd.

"Because, without a name, how can we tell we've seen a thing?" replied
the Knight.

"So you can tell it apart?" confirmed Curd.

"Precisely. So what good is it if both of you call yourselves by the same
names? How can I tell who is who?" asked Sir Rush.

"Oh," stammered Curd, realising at last, "those aren't our names! I'm
Curd the Lion and this is Pilgrim Crow."

"That's better!" said the Knight. "Introductions for starters; pleasantries
for afters."

Sir Rush pulled a flask from a pouch on the back of his saddle, and offered them a drink.

"Now, you say you are lost," said the Knight.

"Yes, we are trying to reach the Southern end of Holywood," said Pilgrim.

"Easily done," said the Knight, pulling a compass from his pouch. "Let
me see, now. South? Is that the blue end or the red end of the needle? I
never can remember. Red sounds hotter: so we'll go that way."

They plodded along behind Sir Rush, now mounted on his Kalandar, and
holding the compass before him. As they marched along, Curd noticed a
soft pitter-pattering noise following them.

"It's not that Barguest again, is it?" Curd whispered.

All paused. The pitter-patter continued, growing stronger as they listened,

until it was a low steady drumming echoing through the trees.

Suddenly Sir Rush burst out laughing. "That's no Barguest; it's just rain!"

"That means we must be getting warmer," said Curd. "It wasn't raining when we entered the wood; it was all ice and snow."

"And that means that we are going in the right direction," said Sir Rush, "it gets warmer as you go south."

The shower soon stopped, and before long they reached the edge of the wood.

"Here we are," said the Knight. "But is this the South? I can't see for that blinding light," he added, parting the branches and squinting out into bright sunshine.

He popped his head back into the shadows as Pilgrim reassured him it really was south. The bright sun was melting the remaining snow, which lay in patches on the ground, and dripped heavily from the trees.

Sweeney and O'Flattery aren't here, though," said Pilgrim. "That means we've won the race."

"Do you mean there are more of you funny little creatures running loose in my wood?" asked Sir Rush.

"Yes, our friends, a Hyena and a Snake," replied Curd the Lion.

"A Snake? Then we must help them, Kalandar, dear, mustn't we?" Sir Rush patted the creature's neck as it hissed in a tongue even O'Flattery would have found strange.

"Oh dear, oh dear," muttered the Knight, stroking his magnificent moustache, "the Minorbore."

"The Minorbore?" asked Curd, " What's that?"

"The MINORBORE?" repeated Sir Rush. "Oh, a terrible bully. If he gets them in his clutches, there's no telling what he will do. Quickly, Kalandar, dear, we must find them."

"But how?" asked Pilgrim.

"Kalandar will lead us to them; won't you, dear," answered the Knight.

"How?" asked Curd.

"I'll send him," replied the good Knight.

"But, just sending him is no good," objected Curd.

"He goes where he's sent, and he scents where he goes," said Sir Rush, firmly. "He'll sniff them out, don't you worry."

"But how can he know the way?" continued Curd.

"He just knows, that's all," Sir Rush replied gently.

"But how?" persisted the ever-inquisitive Curd.

"Because he has the nose for it!" chuckled the Knight. "Hop up, dear creature, and we'll find your friends."

He offered his rein-hand to Curd, who jumped onto the Kalandar's back, clinging tightly to Sir Rush's saddle. "You stay here, Dickie, in case they arrive while we're gone" said the Knight to Pilgrim as they turned to go.

"Dickie?" said Curd and Pilgrim together.

"You are a bird, aren't you?" said the Knight.

"I'm a Crow!" replied Pilgrim, ruffling his feathers, "Pilgrim Crow."

"Pilgrim," repeated the Knight to himself several times as the Kalandar strode away into the darkness of the wood.

"Dickie, indeed!" Pilgrim said to himself, as he glowered at the white locks of the good Knight gradually greying into the gloom.

Waiting for Sir Rush to find Sweeney and O'Flattery, Pilgrim stared out across the field. The setting sun was shining brightly on the rocky ridge to the east, so that it stood out sharply against the darkening sky.

The lengthening shadows of the wood stretched halfway across the field, and the sun was shining on a blue stile-gate on the far side, seeming to beckon him on.

Why don't I go on a little scouting trip to spy out the best route to the rocks while we are waiting? he said to himself, to keep himself company.

He had barely taken a step out of the bushes when a loud croak nearby made him dive back into cover. He peered out from the leaves to see a huge black crow landing on a small molehill in the field.

The crow croaked again, and then dozens of crows started gathering the field. They came from all directions, and assembled in a long rank, and filed across the field in the most extraordinary military manoeuvres, hopping and strutting along together as if ordered to search every last corner of the field.

Pilgrim was convinced that he must have been spotted. But then, as suddenly as they had arrived, the crows flocked together and flew away.

CHAPTER 13

Pilgrim thought, I'll catch them up and pretend to be one of them. I'll spy on them to see if I can learn where Old Corbie the Raven has his nest.

And he flew off in hot pursuit.

CHAPTER FOURTEEN. **The Labyrinth.**

Meanwhile, Sweeney the Heenie and O'Flattery the Snake had decided to go on the other, left hand, path, to try and reach the southern end of the wood first.

As they ventured deeper along their chosen path, the wood seemed to take on a sinister air. The canopy of leaves grew more dense; the path closed almost into a tunnel. They were forced to follow where it led; first circling one way, then the other, with sharp turns between, so that they had no idea which way they were going.

"Let's go back," suggested O'Flattery.

"What? And admit defeat?" said Sweeney. "And whose idea was it to go it alone?"

"Pilgrim's," said O'Flattery.

"Oh, but wasn't it you said: 'You be leader, Sweeney, me lad. Don't you put up with dat Lions-is-best nonsense', eh?"

"Be quiet!" snapped O'Flattery.

They followed the narrow path in silence, wondering whether they hadn't let Curd take the right path after all. As the path snaked this way and that, the darkness grew so that they could see nothing, and had to fumble from tree to tree.

Suddenly Sweeney brightened up. "Have you noticed how we seem to be goin' in circles?" he asked.

"I had noticed," said O'Flattery, "dat we appear to be gettin' nowhere."

"We're nearly dere," said Sweeney.

"Nearly nowhere? I suppose you know where nowhere is?" O'Flattery said bitterly.

"Not far now," replied Sweeney, "dem circles are becoming smaller all de time."

"Blindly going round in ever-decreasing circles to nowhere. I can just see myself telling Curd..."

"Here we are!" burst out Sweeney. "Daylight - just around dis corner!"

With these words ringing in his ears, and he clinging to Sweeney's ears, O'Flattery was suddenly pitched from darkness into blinding light as Sweeney the Heenie galloped forward. As suddenly he found himself pitched to the ground with a thump as Sweeney stopped in his tracks.

There, in a clearing before them, upon a black and white chequerboard floor, bathed in a light which seemed to come from nowhere, sat a huge fat thing with a bull's head, holding an enormous two-headed axe across its lap. Leaning against a tree to the creature's left stood a circular ringed shield with a sharp spike on its central boss.

"Bedad!" gasped Sweeney in amazement.

The beast sat staring into space.

"What class of creature is dat?" asked Sweeney.

"I don't know," whispered O'Flattery, "but I don't like de look of it at all."

"Do you t'ink that it's alive? It doesn't seem to be paying us any heed," said Sweeney, gingerly approaching the statuesque creature.

"Why should I?" bellowed the beast. "Service first; payment after. You haven't served me with an introduction; so why should I pay you any heed? If you are not more polite, I'll serve you with my axe, and you'll pay with your heads!"

"Oh, yes, your Honour! Certainly Sor! Sweeney de Heenie, Sor. And dis fine gentlyman is O'Flattery de Snake. At your service, Sor." Sweeney bowed low.

"And whom may we have de honour of addressing, your Honour?" asked O'Flattery.

"Easy. I am the Great and Terrible Minorbore, and you are in my Maze," roared the beast, resting its axe again.

"Can you tell us, Great and Terrible Minorbore, de way out'a dis maze?" asked Sweeney.

"Of course I can," retorted the Great and Terrible Minorbore, "but I won't. Now it's my turn, and the first question I am going to axe is.."

"Axe?" queried Sweeney, "You mean ask. You ask a question.."

"When I say axe, I mean AXE!" the Minorbore replied. "I AXE a question, and if you cannot answer it, I AXE you again, with this!" it snorted,

slapping the axe-head with its hand. "You may ask a question, but I..."

"Why, t'ank you," Sweeney quickly interrupted, "I WILL ask a question, since you say I may. How do we get out of dis maze?"

"Unfair! Grossly unfair!" roared the Minorbore. "You're twisting my talk around.”

“No more than you did. And you must answer my question,” chuck-led Sweeney, rubbing his paws together gleefully, “how do we get of dis maze?”

O’Flattery looked at Sweeney, and then at the Minorbore. The more he looked, the more he didn’t like the look of it at all. It looked to him as if its talk were about to turn into something altogether more terrible; its face was so contorted with wrath.

After a minute, the Minorbore’s anger subsided, and a deep guttural laughter took its place. “Very well. A good challenge whets my appetite. You will escape the maze by winning this riddling contest. If you win, I show you the way out. If you lose, well then…”

The Minorbore started whetting its axe.

“Now DAT’S unfair!” cried Sweeney.

“My turn. You’ll never answer this one. This is my question. What is the answer? Ha, ha, ha.” The Minorbore bellowed with laughter.

“What?” asked Sweeney, in surprise.

“Eh? How did you know?” asked the beast. “‘What’ IS the answer. Hrmph! I don’t usually have to go any further than that one. Your turn.” grumbled the Bore.

Sweeney was even more surprised when he realised he had stumbled upon the answer, but now settled down to the game with enthusiasm.

“What is made longer by being cut at both ends?” he asked, confident that the Minorbore didn’t read Christmas cracker-puzzles.

“Um… a rope? A pole?” muttered the Minorbore.

“Wrong, wrong!” said Sweeney, “I win.”

“That wasn’t my answer, I was just digging…” growled the Bore, “I was just… A DITCH!” The Minorbore relaxed again, and said:

“My first, in the greeting, ‘hello’,
But not in a ‘how do ye do?’
My second is in what follows,
But not in what’s behind you.
An insect, ever-so-small-oh,
Brings a sting in the end you’ll rue.”

“What could be first in de greeting ‘hello’, dat’s not in a ‘how do ye do’?” whispered O’Flattery nervously. “Could it be a greetings card, he means, do you t’ink? A ‘hello’ letter?”

“Letter?” repeated Sweeney. “That’s it! What letter is in ‘hello’ dat’s not in ‘how do ye do’?”

“L?” replied O’Flattery.

“De very same,” said Sweeney, “L is de first letter of de word we want.

Now, de second letter must be in 'what follows', but not in 'what walks behind you'; and DAT," he cried triumphantly, "is F!"

"L.... F?" muttered O'Flattery. "I never heard of a word dat started wid dem two letters. F.... L. Well now, dem letters has an honourable pedigree to my certain knowledge, and I personally knows a few people called after dem fine letters."

"O'Flattery! Oh, prattley." sighed Sweeney. "Let's get on wid de last part: de ever-so-small-oh insect dat brings a sting in de tail you'll rue."

"A Bee-in-your-bonnet? A Wasp-in-a-wig?" suggested O'Flattery helpfully. "Ants-in-the-pants?"

"Ants! Of course!" shouted Sweeney.

"But Sweeney, L and F and Ants doesn't make a word," objected O'Flattery.

"Dat's it!" howled Sweeney in delight. "L-F-ant: elephant! Isn't dat right Mr. Minorbore, Sor?"

"Yes, I suppose," the disgruntled Minorbore mumbled.

"My turn," said Sweeney. "De more I grow; de less you see of me."

"Grow... grow..." said the Minorbore. "Elephant? Elephant-in-the-dark? No... DARK! Eh, that was easy. Now for my last riddle! You won't guess this one in a year and a day."

The Minorbore licked its finger and tested the sharpness of its axe-blade.

"Why is a Wren-drive like a Sat-king?" said the Minorbore, tossing its head with glee.

"Er... er..." stuttered Sweeney.

The Minorbore guffawed and swung its axe to the ready.

"Why is it?" hissed O'Flattery urgently.

"I don't know," said Sweeney, "You t'ink of something."

"I have. Let's go," whispered O'Flattery.

The Minorbore's eyes flickered with a strange delight as it slowly stood up, swinging its axe like pendulum of a clock.

"Tick-tock. Tick-tock.

CHAPTER 14

Your time is up," he chanted. "My blade is keen to axe you.."

He advanced on them, his great axe glinting as he swung it over his head.

"Halt!"

A shout from behind Sweeney stopped the Minorbore's advance for a moment, and in that instant a white phantom appeared.

"Release my friends," ordered Sir Rush as he jabbed the Minorbore with his lance.

The Minorbore backed away. "That's not an answer," it protested.

"No," replied Sir Rush, "But it gets straight to the point."

The Minorbore glared at Sir Rush. Sir Rush stared back.

Suddenly a familiar voice appeared out of the impasse: "Come on you two, jump up!"

It was Curd the Lion! Their friendly little Lion, their helpful little Lion, their own Curd the Lion, Leader of their Great Adventure, come to his crew's aid.

Sweeney and O'Flattery scrambled up to join Curd in the saddle. The Knight persuaded the Minorbore to sit down with a jab of his lance before leaving the maze.

"Do you t'ink he'll try to chase us?" asked Sweeney, as the Kalandar threaded its way through the maze without stopping.

"He'd like to," replied Sir Rush, "because once he starts a-riddling, he never gives up. He makes you go round and round in circles and drives you round the bend, so to speak. That's why he's called the Minor-Bore. The trick is not to answer at all but leave immediately, because he won't leave the maze without his Barguest beast. I make sure I keep the Barguest on the run and away from the maze. For if the Minorbore rides out on his Barguest Beast – that's Serious! Even I may not be a match for them then, even with my dear Kalandar Steed."

With those words Sir Rush set off with Curd, Sweeney and O'Flattery sitting on the Kalandar's back to reunite them with Pilgrim Crow at the South end of Holywood.

As they rode along, Sweeney and O'Flattery told Curd all about the Minorbore and his strange riddling contest and how he kept trying to cheat so that he could AXE their heads off.

This axe made a deep impression on Curd, who hoped he would never have to face the Bore on his own, because what he did know was that he was no good at riddles. Like jokes and rabbits, they were tricksy, and just as you thought you were going to catch one, it would dart sideways from under you, leaving you looking more stupid than if you'd never tried to get it in the first place.

Sir Rush and the Animals reached the Southern edge of Holywood.

"Where's Pilgrim?" they all asked as the Kalandar drew to a halt.

"Are you sure dis is where you left him? asked Sweeney as they dismounted.

At that moment a fluttering and crashing of branches announced Pilgrim Crow's safe return.

The good Knight interrupted a clamour of voices, demanding to know where he'd been and what had happened to him. "Now that we have you all together, Sirs, I will depart to hunt the Barguest."

As he made his farewells, the Knight said: "Be brave; lose not faith, sirs.

If you need my help, I'll defend you in the trials of your coming Adventure."

"My Gallant Knight, let justice do the rest," replied Pilgrim gallantly, as he bowed low and grandly swept his hat across the ground in front of him, Cavalier-fashion. "Sirrah, adieu."

"It's not Sir Rah, it's Sir Rush," said Curd quietly.

Curd went to the Knight, who bent down to him as he whispered: "Do you think we'll succeed in finding Mum's Brooch?"

The gentle Knight whispered back confidentially: "Well, there's no way of knowing, but I'll have 'alf a bet that you will."

The Knight sat up again, turned his charger, and rode into the darkness to resume his hunt to keep the Minorbore and his Barguest apart.

The Animals turned to Pilgrim, who was standing, cap in hand, gazing after the knight.

They saw him now in a new light: he too was BALD. His bare pate shone like a halo above his black-feathered head. He was tonsured, like a monk. So that's what he kept under his hat!

A chorus of voices chanted in unison: "Where on earth have you been?"

"I flew after the crows," said Pilgrim. "I thought they might lead me to the Great Raven. But they didn't. Instead…"

CHAPTER FOURTEEN & A HALF.   **Pilgrim's Progress.**

The crows, pursued by Pilgrim, flew directly to the rocks and rested there.

By the time Pilgrim arrived, they had gone. He flew to the place he had last seen them, and landed on a high flat-topped rock, shaped like an old school writing desk, or lectern. While he was here, he thought, he would have a look around for the Corbie-stone.

Suddenly a voice rang out behind him, giving him such a start that he fell off the writing desk rock and only just stopped himself tumbling right down the cliff.

He looked up. Before him he saw a most peculiar bird. It had two heads, short stubby wings, a stout body, short legs and greyish scales instead of feathers, which shone iridescent in the rays of the evening sun. It was singing as it waddled along:

"The Dodo never stood a chance,
For it trusted all and sundry;
It hardly took a second glance
When into a man it blundry.
Its only fault was ignorance
That that man was hungry.

When it met that hungry man
The dodo barely blinked;
It never flew, (not that it can),
No danger with that man it linked.
It is because it never ran
The Dodo is extinct."

At that moment, the strange bird saw Pilgrim. Its two heads looked at one another and then turned to him and affably introduced themselves:
"Do call me Nid…"
"Nod is my name."
"Are you a NID-NOD then?" Pilgrim asked, "or a Dodo, perhaps?"
"A Dodo? Good heavens, no…"
"…nothing so common as that!"
"We is a DODONGS!'" they chimed together, "We rings the changes."
"I rings out the old…"

"…and I rings in the new."

"We plays it by y-ear!" Their voices indeed rang pleasantly together, like musical bells. Changing their tune, they turned to Pilgrim with a serious air and asked him a riddle:

"If I remove sunbeams from its scales…"

"…with what extinct wind-bag am I left, chasing its tail?"

Before Pilgrim could say a word, the Dodongs started singing:

"Do- Ray- Me- Fa-…"

"…So- La- Te- Do."

"Take away So-La and Ray…"

"…and add the head to the tail, chasing itself: Do-Do…"

"…and what do you have?"

"Me-Fa-Te-Do-Do, right?"

"Me farty Dodo. Extinct wind-bag…"

"…Musical scales, see?"

Pilgrim nodded dumbly. The two heads continued happily:

"Speaking of scales…"

"…I have scales…"

"…instead of feathers…"

"…the better to make music!"

As they spoke and moved, their tiny shiny scales jingled pleasantly like little bells.

"…and because scales…"

"…are better for balancing."

"Why?" asked Pilgrim.

"Just is," replied both heads together.

"You mean just ARE," Pilgrim corrected them. "Scales just ARE better for balancing. But anyway, you can't say JUST IS, you must give a proper reason why."

The Dodongs looked at each other for a moment, then spoke in turn:

"Did you ever hear…"

"…of a better balanced pair of scales…"

"…than the scales of Justice?"

"And, as for a reason…"

"…Justice and Reason go hand in hand"

"But, but…" stammered Pilgrim.

"What better reason than justice?" they demanded.

"Well, err…" Pilgrim started, only to be interrupted again.

"If that's not reason enough," they added:

"Just IS…"

"…being purely as it is…"

"...needs no further..."

"...just-IF-ication!"

Pilgrim was now at loss for words. The queer bird looked at him, as if expecting some remark, then said:

"I declare!"

"Birds of a feather..."

"...should stick together!"

"I do."

"But you haven't any feathers," Pilgrim protested.

"That PROVES it!" they shouted.

"Proves what?" Pilgrim shouted back pluckily, certain he had caught them out this time, "and what about your tail, eh?"

But they refused to be drawn, and declared, quite unruffled:

"Well..."

"...that's another story."

Seeing his bewilderment, the Dodongs added, sympathetically:

"That's why I have two heads."

"Two heads are better than one."

"Why are two heads better than one?" argued Pilgrim, "I should become confused with two heads."

"And what happens when you become confused?"

"Why, you quite lose your head..."

"...and that's the end of you!"

"Look at the Dodo. The end of the race for him, it was..."

"...whereas I..."

"...can lose my head..."

"...and still keep ahead!" chirped both together.

"What are you doing here, anyway?"

"Are you a Fugitive?"

"I was following the crows,. I'm looking for a Raven, you see," Pilgrim began, only to be rudely interrupted by another of their riddles:

"Whom did the brave Crow fight..."

"...on the six steps he took to his nest?"

"I don't know," Pilgrim replied wearily.

"Why, the Brat, of course!"

"Take six steps from Crow to Nest..."

"...changing one letter of the word..."

"...at each step, and you'll see."

Before Pilgrim had time to work it out, the bird asked another question:

"Talking of nests.."

"…have you seen a Symmetree, hereabouts?…"

"…A Symmetree is the only refuge…"

"…in which I can safely nest to lay our eggs."

"Why only in a Symmetree?" asked Pilgrim.

The Dodongs glanced shiftily from side to side, then whispered confidentially:

"SNAKES!"

"…poisonous Snakes!"

"But can't snakes climb Symmetrees?" Pilgrim asked, "Some snakes are very good tree-climbers."

The Dodongs considered this gravely for a minute:

"Of course not!"

"Did you ever hear of a snake that climbed STRAIGHT up a tree?"

"No. When a snake climbs…"

"…it wiggles and winds its way around the tree-trunk, one way or the other…"

"…and THAT breaks the Symmetree…"

"…and the snake falls down, straightaway!"

"But what would happen if a snake did manage to climb?" Pilgrim persisted.

The Dodongs began to fret. Looking at each other queerly, it answered with another question:

"What do you get from a Symmetree?"

Why snakes can't climb a Symmetree

"SymmeTREACLE, of course!"

"And that's a Sovereign Remedy…"

"…against snake-bite."

"But," objected Pilgrim, "Symmetrical isn't a remedy for anything - it's a Description!"

"Precisely what I said…"

"…a Prescription - the very best tonic for snake-bite."

"But the word is SymmeTRICAL," Pilgrim insisted.

"Sometimes a trickle…"

"…sometimes a flood."

"It depends on the weather…"

"…whether it is, or whether it isn't."

Pilgrim gave up trying to argue with this crass creature, and asked: "What makes you think there might be a Symmetree around here?"

"Oh, that's easy."

"Brimstone and Treacle always go together…"

"...so we've come here to the Brimstones..."

"...to find the Treacle..."

"...Really..."

"...you are ignorant!"

"But we don't mind."

"Not at all. Now, as you were saying..."

"Saying?" asked PIlgrim.

"Asking then,"

"No need to be tetchy,"

"Asking about a Raven, you was..."

"We knows him, we do." The two heads nodded triumphantly. Pilgrim didn't know what to say.

"Ask us, then..."

"...and we'll tell you..."

"...sure as eggs is eggs."

"Where does he live?" asked Pilgrim.

"Talk about blunt!" said Nid.

"Could't get much blunter than that," said Nod.

"To the point," said Nid.

"Shall we?" said Nod.

"Yes, let's," said Nid.

"He lives," said both together, "on this very ridge what we are standing on."

"Not a thousand yards..." said Nid.

"A hundred."

"Not a hundred yards from here. On the Corbie Stone."

"But you won't find it..."

"Not unless you go much further..."

"South..."

"To the very end of the ridge..."

"And look back."

"And there you'll see that ancient rock they call the Corbie Stone..."

"Ancient seat of the Great Raven, Old Corbie."

"Yes," said Pilgrim Crow eagerly, "and..."

"That's it!"

"Time's up!"

The Dodongs became suddenly crochety as it dismissively waved aside any more questions with a wild counterpointing of their wings, which whirled about like helicopter blades:

"Tempus fugit..."

"...Time presses – must fly!"

The curious bird waddled away down the path, trilling to itself in a quavering voice.

"In repartee,"

"if you would be,"

"as E. Clerihew, droll,"

"heed... ... ..."

Pilgrim didn't catch the rest of this rhyme, for it was caught upon a gust of wind, and faded away with the Dodongs itself over the hill.

By then the light, too, was fading fast, and Pilgrim flew as fast as he could back towards Holywood before dusk fell.

CHAPTER FIFTEEN.   **Doubles and Duels.**

As Pilgrim finished his tale, Curd remarked: "What a strange bird the Dodongs must be, with his two heads an' all."

"Yes, a class of Razorbill, I'd say," laughed Sweeney, "judging by de close shave you had, Pilgrim."

"What, me?" Pilgrim hastily restored his hat to his bald head, and bustled about busily to restore his lost dignity. "Yes, well… It's time we were off. It's nearly dark now, and safe to cross the field."

"Did you hear dat?" O'Flattery asked Sweeney under his breath.

"Yes I did. Dat means we knows where to go now, once Pilgrim shows us where dat ridge is," whispered Sweeney the Heenie.

"So we don't need Mudder Beanie, no more," said O'Flattery, "Nor do we need dat Cup no more, neither. I'm fed up wid carryin' it."

"Wait, don't chuck it away, yet," said Sweeney, "not until we get dere. Just in case Mudder Beanie was trickin' us. Den we still got what Ole Corbie wants, eh?"

"You're right," said O'Flattery, "I'll hang onto it den."

The Animals set out across the field in the last rays of the setting sun. Their shadows reached out towards the stile-gate ahead of them and climbed over first, disappearing into the deeper shadows of the farm track cast by high stone walls on either side.

So that was the wisdom which Pilgrim always kept under his hat! thought Curd. No wonder he kept it hidden. He was still deep in thought as he trotted round a bend and stopped dead.

"Riddle-me, riddle-me, riddle-me-ree!"

He froze. Straight ahead on the track, stood the Barguest. Its eyes blazed; its steely trap-jaw gaped wide. On its back, the bull-headed Minorbore sat tall, wielding its huge double-bladed axe. They were trapped!

"Answer my riddle, and you shall go free," shouted the Bore, "I've axed you once, and I've axed you again; if I axe you thrice, you'll feel the pain!"

Curd shivered.

The Barguest's staring goggley eyes numbed them with fright as only a Terror-Bogie numbs. Never was so grim a brute borne on its back as the Minorbore, grunting and chuntering to itself. Step by step they bore down on the Animals.

The Minorbore halted right in front of them and bellowed: "Why is a Wren-drive like a Sat-king?"

117

All eyes turned to Sweeney the Heenie, Champion of the Plain Man and Conqueror of Conundrums.

Sweeney lowered his head in shame. "I forgot at dis precise moment de answer to dat particular riddle, Sor. Would you like to try me on another one, perhaps?"

With a loud snort the Minorbore raised its axe high, dug its heels sharply into the Barguest's flanks and the great shaggy hound lurched forward.

From the darkness behind the little Animals came a piercing whistle.

They all turned at once. It was Sir Rush! But how changed? Gone were the white armour and long white hair. His head, now completely bald, shone like a full moon over the black lake of his breastplate, on which gleamed, like rippling reflections, these golden letters: "Ye Blakke Knyghte of Brimastane".

The Minorbore hesitated; the Barguest pawed at the ground.

Curd and his friends scrambled out of harm's way next to the rough stone

walls on one side of the track.

"This night you will Rue, O Brimstone Brag!" shouted Sir Rush.
Sir Rush and the Minorbore sat astride their chargers, facing each other.
Slowly, Sir Rush lowered his lance until it was pointing straight at the Minorbore. The Minorbore raised his great axe high over his head with both
hands. Like a bad omen, its blade glinted blood red in the last rays of the
sun.

"Come on, Sir Rush!" shouted Curd.

"Jab him… Poke him… Knock him off!" Sweeney, O'Flattery and Pilgrim
spurred him on.

The Kalandar and the Barguest both lurched forward and the great beasts
thundered together. Sparks, stones and dust flew!

"KERRANG!" The Minorbore's first blow rang like a gong on Sir Rush's
shield, echoing down the walls as they parted.

Turning, they bore down on each other at tremendous speed, the Barguest baying and the Kalandar hissing like a steam train along the track.

Axe clashed on shield again, splitting it so that the two halves clattered to the ground as they parted for the second time.

"Oh dear," squeaked O'Flattery, "de Minorbore's winning."

Bellowing and baying, the Minorbore and Sir Rush charged once again into clouds of dust so thick Curd could barely see who was who.

"KERRRUMP!" The bellowing abruptly ceased and the baying turned into an anguished howl.

Sir Rush rode triumphant out of the cloud with the Minorbore's great Bull-head impaled upon his lance!

"Awful," cried Pilgrim, "I can barely bear to look. He's beheaded the Minorbore!"

All eyes settled upon the dwindling dust cloud.

Slowly from the murk emerged the swarthy shape of the Barguest-dog. On its back, where before the Barguest bore the now-beheaded Minorbore, sat a fat and bawling baby boy.

Sir Rush rode up to the blubbering new-borne babe, took the Barguest's reins, and led the bewildered beast back up the track to the spot where the astonished animals sat upon the walls.

"Sir Nigel Rush, Ye Blakke Knyghte of Brimastane, at your service!" announced the brave black knight.

"How did you do it?" a chorus of voices asked as Sir Rush raised his

Bull-headed trophy high in the air on his lance.

"Impenetrability!" answered Sir Rush. "Impenetrability is the key."

"What do you mean?" asked Pilgrim.

"In the dark of night what is more impenetrable than complete blackness?" said the Knight.

"Er, nothing, I suppose," said Pilgrim.

"Exactly! Hence my wonderful new suit of armour," said the Knight, clashing his mailed fist upon his breastplate. "And my gorgeous black hair," he added, stroking the air around his bald pink head. "My blackness made me Impenetrable in the dark! So the Minorbore couldn't possibly hurt me!"

Sir Rush turned to go, leading the sobbing babe, seated upon its shaggy dog, down the track towards Holywood.

"Well, Sirs, I must be going upon my way and you upon yours, adieu!" As the strange procession rounded a bend in the track, Sweeney turned to the others. "Some Minorbore!" he laughed, "T'was only a great big baby, so it was!"

"It fooled you," said Curd.

"It did not so," said Sweeney, "I just played along wid it dere."

"Well, just come along with us here, now," said Pilgrim Crow, as he led the way along the track.

The clouds were darkening the moon more often now, and all the animals were tired.

"Can we have a rest, soon?" asked Curd.

"There's a barn up ahead," said Pilgrim Crow, who had flown that way when he followed the crows. "It's at the end of this track. It's not far."

Slipping through the gate at the track's end, the animals found themselves in an open field again. As far as they could see in the poor light, the farm track continued across that wide-open field. They would have to figure out how to cross that in the morning. Right now they were all too tired. To their left, the great bulk of the barn loomed uninvitingly.

"Here we are!" said Pilgrim, "We can rest in there."

Curd looked up into the entrance of the barn, yawning hollow as if filled with a deep hunger for the little travellers.

"Come in," said Pilgrim, as he entered the great emptiness.

"Come in… come in…come in…" echoed the barn's deep throat, until the sound was completely swallowed in the darkness.

"I don't like the look of it," said Curd nervously, "couldn't we rest out here?"

"What? And be seen at first light by the crows?" scoffed Pilgrim.

"Hey, here's some straw," said Sweeney the Heenie, who had ventured into the barn while the others argued. "It's quite safe."

"Safe... safe.... safe..." echoed the barn reassuringly.

Curd was too tired to argue. They hadn't rested since leaving Old Queen Mumbie's home, and he was glad after all to flop into the bed of warm hay.

"If I hadn't seen it with my own eyes," Curd's voiced piped up in the dark, "I'd never have believed in that Barguest. I'd have said it was just a shaggy-dog story."

"And I would'na believed in dat Minorbore, neither," said Sweeney the Heenie, not to be outdone, "and dat riddle, now, de one about de Wren-drive and de Sat King. What's dat all about, now?"

"I don't know," said Curd, picturing the dreaded Minorbore with his giant two-head axe and shuddering.

" Did you ever hear de one about…" started O'Flattery.

"Be quiet."

Soon the barn was buzzing with snores as the animals dropped off to sleep one by one, wondering what adventures the next day would bring.

CHAPTER SIXTEEN.   **A Rough Ride.**

Sir Rush, upon his Kalandar, holding the reins of the Barguest and the once-proud Minorbore in his hand, arrived at the stile-gate at the lower end of the walled track.

As he leaned far over in his saddle to reach for the bolt, the Minorbabe seized its chance and spurred the Barguest forward. Barging the Kalandar, the Barguest knocked Sir Rush out of his saddle onto his head. As the Barguest battled the Kalandar, the Minorbabe leaped down and tied the dizzy Knight to the gatepost with his own belt and braces.

Snatching up its great Bull-head, the Minorbore resumed its reign and mount and rode off in pursuit of the Animals.

"Riddle-me, riddle-me, riddle-me-ree!" In a blaze of light that filled the barn door, the Minorbore stood in all its fury, axe in hand. Curd sat in a daze, blinded by the light and pure panic. What could he do? There was no escape this time.

"Why is a Wren-drive like a Sat-King?" The dreaded riddle rang in his ears like a Sentence. Without an answer, he knew just how that Sentence would be pronounced: "Off with his head!"

He remembered the words of advice on Henry's bedroom wall –"If you can keep your head, when all about you are losing theirs" – and thought of running. But where? Oh, what was the answer? What was the answer?...

Curd awoke with a start. It was just a dream. The Minorbore wasn't here after all.

The sun was blazing in his eyes through a chink in the wall-planks of the barn. Curd rushed to the chink and squinted into the broad daylight outside.

It was a grand morning. Little clouds were scudding about their business across the broad highways of the sky, delivering a packet of rain here, and hoisting a shady umbrella there. The air fizzed with an invigorating freshness, and the wind played through Curd's shaggy mane with tickly fingers.

He wondered whether in the light of such a lovely day, all the strange adventures of the previous night had not been just a frightening dream, a....

The cloudy spottiness of the sky seemed to be spreading like a rash. At an alarming speed the little black clouds were winging their way hither and thither, contradicting the wind.

"Get up, quickly!" he whispered urgently, withdrawing his head from the crack in the wall. "Crows! The sky's full of them!"

"How are we going to escape?" they asked, gathering round to peer out.

124

As far as they could see outside, the broad field around the barn offered no shelter from the hungry eyes of the Great Raven's horde.

"We can't run for it," said Pilgrim, "they would catch us in no time."

"Let's stay here till dey've gone," said the ever-cautious O'Flattery, "dey're bound to get fed up sooner or later."

"Talking of getting fed up, I'm hungry," said Sweeney.

"How can you think of food at a time like this?" snapped Pilgrim.

"Shh!" Sharp-eared Curd hushed his squabbling companions. Above their chatter and the distant cacophony of crows, he had heard a faint but growing growl.

Running to the chink in the wall, he looked out.

"It's a truck!" he shouted. "And it's coming this way. Hide, quickly!"

The animals dived for cover as the growl grew to a roar and the farm-truck snarled around the corner, sputtering to a halt beside the barn door.

The driver jumped out, walked round to the rear of the truck, and let the tail-gate down with a clatter.

"What's he doing? Is he coming?" asked Sweeney.

Before Curd, who had hidden behind a hay-bale near the door, could answer, the doors swung wide and the solid figure of a farmer entered the barn. His ruddy face glowered over Curd as he bent forward, embraced the bale behind which Curd was hidden, lifted and carried it away, leaving Curd completely exposed.

As Curd dashed to the next bale to join Sweeney, he was suddenly struck by a thought. Hay-bales being loaded onto a wagon meant cattle being fed, and there were no cattle in this field. That meant the truck would have to cross the field to another where the cattle might be. If the truck could carry hay, it could carry a little extra - them - tucked among the bales, safe from prying eyes of crows!

"Quick," he whispered to Sweeney, "one of us must make a dash for the wagon each time he loads another bale of hay. That way we can all escape in the truck."

"Good idea," said Sweeney. "O'Flattery, did you hear?"

"Course I heard, eejit," hissed O'Flattery crossly, "just get on wid it will you, now"

The hissing continued. Curd turned to tell him to shut up when suddenly the hissing turned into a squawk! "Help!"

A clawed paw had O'Flattery by the throat and yanked him off Sweeney's back into the shadows.

The cracked Cup he had stolen from Queen Mumbie-Bumbee flew from his coils and bounced across the bales.

"What the... rats!" cried Curd.

Sweeney leaped towards the rat, straight into Pilgrim and knocked off his hat.

"Grab him!" Curd grabbed O'Flattery's disappearing head with one paw and the rat holding him with his other claw and heaved backwards, dragging the pair of them out into daylight.

Sweeney pounced down onto the rat holding O'Flattery. The rat let go and fled back into the shadows just as the farmer returned for his second bale.

Curd and Sweeney clapped each other on the back in triumph.

The farmer picked up the bale and turned to go. Snatching his hat, Pilgrim whispered, "follow me," as he walked close behind the bulky farmer as he stumped across the yard under his heavy load.

The farmer heaved the bale into the truck and as he returned to fetch the next bale, Pilgrim, Curd and Sweeney scrambled onto a bale left on

the ground, jumped onto the tail-gate and into the covered back, hiding
behind the bales. O'Flattery wriggled out after them just as a group of rats
emerged from between the bales in the barn.

"Wait for me!" O'Flattery reared his head up to climb the tailgate but
there was nothing for him to cling to. Sweeney leaped down and grabbed
O'Flattery in his teeth, flicked him into the back on the truck, jumped onto
the bale and onto the tail-gate, just managing to roll out of harm's way
as the last of the bales thumped down beside him and the tail-gate was
slammed shut.

Just then dozens of pairs of yellow eyes, glowering balefully, appeared in
all the cracks between the wallboards of the barn.

The truck sputtered into life. With a cough, roar and shudder, it reversed
out of the yard and drove off, bumping along the rough track across the
field.

"Drat!" A furious King Ziggu rose to his full height, growling to his assembled rat-multitude: "We can't follow that truck. But we'll catch up with
them yet. I know a short-cut."

The Animals peeped out over the tail-gate as the truck sped south. The
barn jumped and jerked into the distance. On their right they could see the
grim out-jutting rocks of Brimstone on the skyline.

127

"Sweeney, Sweeney," whispered O'Flattery. "It's gone!"

"What?"

"De Cup. It's gone. I must've dropped it when dat rat grabbed me."

"What? Dey must have it den," growled Sweeney, "Widout de Secret we're ruined! Why didn't you say so back dere?"

"I forgot. I didn't notice in all de excitement," wailed O'Flattery.

"What are you two bickering about now?" asked Pilgrim Crow. "Ouch! What the...?"" He took it off and looked inside. "What's this? Something hard."

Pilgrim felt inside. He pulled out the Cup, cracked but not broken.

"Where did that come from?" said Curd the Lion, "Hey, that's Queen Mumbie's cracked cup, isn't it?"

"Why so it is," said Pilgrim Crow. They both looked at O'Flattery the Snake and Sweeney the Heenie, who were grinning sheepishly.

"You stole it," said Pilgrim.

"We borrowed it, sort of," started Sweeney. "It belongs to Old Corbie, you know."

"And we're taking it back..." continued O'Flattery.

"In exchange for our jewelled Brooch," added Sweeney.

"But it's Queen Mumbie's," said Curd.

"She stole it," said Sweeney, "Mother Beanie said so."

"And she told us de Secret of where de Brooch is hid," said O'Flattery, "so give me de Cup back or you'll never find out."

"And you believed her," said Curd, "after she tipped me in the water?"

"She's a good friend of his. She knows," said O'Flattery.

"Ok. Where is it hid?" asked Pilgrim.

"Give it me first," replied O'Flattery.

"Oh, give it to him," said Curd, "but mind you don't lose it again until we can give it back."

"Agreed," said O'Flattery, chuckling under his breath to Sweeney, "I didn't say to whom," and out loud, "Oh, and Sweeney de Heenie here is goin' to be de leader from now on."

"Why?" asked Pilgrim.

"Because we has de Secret of where de Brooch is hid," replied O'Flattery, "and widout dat, you're nuttin', you're goin' nowhere. And we're not tellin' less Sweeney's leader, see."

"But I'm the leader," said Curd, "you said so, Pilgrim."

"True," said Pilgrim, "But he's right. All I know is what the Dodongs told me: that the Corbie stone can only be seen from the South end of the ridge. He didn't tell me what to do when we got there, though."

"An dat's what we know," cried O'Flattery, "Dat is, what Sweeney only knows. And he's not tellin' till he's de Leader, an even den, only at de right time, when we gets dere."

"How about it then, Curd?" Pilgrim said. "You've been leader up to now. Let Sweeney be leader for a bit, eh? It's only fair really."

"Oh, alright! But you'd better tell us when we get there," said Curd.

"Of course I will," replied Sweeney.

The truck screeched to a halt, knocking the animals backwards into the hay-bales as the farmer jumped out to open a gate. They had barely recovered when he set off again with a ferocious jolt that tumbled them into the tailboards.

"That farmer's face looks familiar," said Curd, "I'm sure I've seen him somewhere before."

"Don't be silly," replied Pilgrim. "You've never been up here before."

"I suppose," agreed Curd, "but all the same…"

The truck drove past some farm-buildings, a pond, and on into a birch-wood standing at the base of the rocks themselves. Reaching its southern edge, the truck stopped at another gate.

This looks like the South end of the ridge," said Pilgrim.

"All out, now!" shouted Sweeney, getting into the swing of leading as they all leaped out together into the heather beside the road.

Pilgrim scouted ahead while the Animals scrambled through the scrub and crevices of the lowermost rocks. He landed on a ledge, high on the rock-face, overhung with a great boulder. Scanning the line of the ridge to the north, he noticed, standing a little proud of the other promontories, a strange flat rock. It had a large heavy beak, and little eyes set back above the beak, like the detached head of some strange bird.

"That's it!" Crowing with delight, he fluttered down to his companions, now struggling up towards him. "I've seen it! I've seen it!" he cawed.

"Where?"

"North," he cried. "If you climb along the ridge to the next outcrop, you will be able to see it clearly from there."

Climbing as quickly as they dared while keeping out of sight of the roving crows, the intrepid Animals crept along the paths through the bilberry-bushes, which covered the ground between the birches below and the bare rocks above like a tufty beard. The black bird-horde still seemed to be concentrating its search on the valley below, but the occasional sudden appearance of a jackdaw in the air immediately above them kept them busy diving in and out of cover.

Reaching at last the next outcrop of rock, they crept forward as far as they dared on their bellies, and peered over. The sight that greeted them was all that they had hoped for.

There it was - the Corbie stone!

Perched above a precipitous cliff, the craggy crow-head looked out over the valley as if surveying its own domain.

The end of their Adventure was in sight!

CHAPTER SEVENTEEN.   **The Stone.**

Kraa!"

The four Adventurers, Sweeney the Heenie and O'Flattery the Snake, Curd the Lion and Pilgrim Crow, lay side-by-side on the bare ledge of rock, staring in wonder at the great Corbie-stone.

"Kraa!"

The sound seemed to come directly from that wonderful head perched upon the cliff-top, as if it had become miraculously alive, issuing commands to the hosts in the sky above.

With each cry, the ragged multitude of crows in the sky seemed to change direction; wheeling and swirling, rising and falling, like wispy columns of smoke, wind-blown across the valley.

"Kraa!"

The Animals felt the sky grow dark as the crows massed towards the ridge in a menacing black thunder-cloud, rattling with their harsh calls.

"Kraa!"

From the Corbie-stone the black form of the Great Raven itself spread its wings, and flapped slowly into the air. The Animals watched it mount majestically upon the warm air-currents rising from the ridge.

From the black cloud, a black rain fell: a rain of crows, tumbling down towards the ridge.

The soaring Raven, huge as it was, disappeared into the seething tumbling mass of crows.

"Kaark! Kaark!"

CHAPTER 17

Curd looked up behind him. A crow was diving straight for the Animals laid on the ledge.

"We've been spotted!" he cried.

"Run!" shouted Sweeney. "Follow me!"

He had seen a deep crack in the rock-face of the next outcrop, which would shelter them if only they could scramble down the slope in time.

The Animals raced forward down the ridge-side, over a broken sheep-wall and down between the rocks to the bottom of the slope.

Crows pecked and clawed at them as they tore across the short distance to the base of the crack.

"Phew, we only just made it," panted Curd as they hurled themselves into the safety of the narrow fissure as the leading birds were forced to veer away from the cliff-face. A beating of wings and a raucous cawing resounded frighteningly in the narrow cleft, but the crows dared not enter.

The floor ahead led steeply inwards and upwards, looking as if it might lead them to the top of the ridge in the direction of the Corbie-stone.

"Come on, let's try it," said the ever-adventurous Sweeney. "We can't go back now, to be sure."

They toiled up the steep and slippery mud-floor of the great fissure, ignoring the noise of the birds outside, and helping one another when they slipped or tripped in the treacherous darkness.

"It's brighter ahead," said Sweeney, "perhaps dere aren't any crows up dere."

"Yes, perhaps we can sneak out unseen at the top," muttered Curd hopefully.

Nearing the top, they discovered another crevice leading back down at a right angle to theirs.

"Dat might be another way out," suggested O'Flattery, thinking that going down looked a lot easier than continuing up, as if he was doing the climbing.

Ignoring him, the animals climbed on. At the very top, the fissure was capped by a large boulder, under which even very small animals would need to squeeze to escape. Sweeney stuck his neck out to see the lie of the land.

"Yeeow!" Two crows lying in ambush seized his big ears with their sharp beaks, and tried to drag him out like a worm.

Sweeney angrily dug his heels in and heaved. He pulled so hard that he dragged the birds into the cave-mouth before ripping himself free. With a yelp of pain, he catapulted backwards into the cave.

"We'll have to try the side exit now," said Pilgrim, as Sweeney nursed his torn ears.

The animals retraced their steps back to the side-crevice, and Pilgrim led the way down it, striding firmly into thin air!

His flapping wings broke his fall, and he re-emerged with only his dignity ruffled.

"What now?" asked Curd.

Just then a dark horde burst into the side-crevice and scurried up towards them. Rats!

"We can't go that way, now!" said Curd.

"Try this way."

From the entrance at the base of the crevice up which they had come, a chilling voice, familiar to Sweeney and O'Flattery, sneered its invitation to go down.

"It's King Ziggu-rat!" said Sweeney, as a second horde of rats pressed into the narrow confines of the cleft.

"Bejapes, we're trapped!" cried O'Flattery.

"We make our last stand here," announced Pilgrim Crow gravely, "and fight to the bitter end."

As the rats streamed up both channels towards the animals, chanting their wicked ratty cries, their King, Ziggu-Rat, shouted," Come along quietly now, and we'll escort you to Old Corbie!"

"Never," snarled Sweeney, "I've a score to settle wid you, Ratty-king!"

Cackling laughter echoing ahead of him, Sweeney charged down the abyss. The Rats stopped in their

tracks, and nervous murmurings rippled through their ranks. The murmurings grew to a loud buzz.

"You don't understand, I…" started the Rat King, but his voice was drowned out by the ear-piercing pitch of a cloud of bees in full battle-fury bearing down on them.

"Fight them, you Rats!" screamed King Zig-gu-rat, as Queen Mumbie-Bumbee and her subjects tore into the tight-packed horde of rats, stinging as they came.

Rats clung to the walls on both sides to escape the barbs of the bees.

Ignoring Curd and his companions standing at the head of the crevice, the terrified rats fled down both clefts in droves, the unstoppable bee-horde herding them along.

"Stand and fi-eeee…!" King Ziggu's voice tailed away to a squeal as he was carried off in the avalanche of fleeing rats.

"Good old Mumbie!" shouted the animals,

clustering around their heroine as she alighted.

"How on earth did you find us, and where did all your subjects spring from?" asked Curd.

"After you'd gone, the heat of the fire got me thinking, and I hatched the idea of my subjects bee-coming to help you. And finding that huge cloud of birds was not hard," replied the Queen, "so here we are!"

As the animals heaped praise on Mumbie, O'Flattery watched in silence. He began to wriggle uncomfortably.

"What's the matter with you?" asked Pilgrim.
Queen Mumbie-Bumbee stared, too, at O'Flattery, a little too hard for comfort.

"Is anything wrong, O'Flattery, dear?" she said. "Is there anything you'd like to tell me?"

"Ahem. Psst!" O'Flattery looked sideways at the Queen. "Your Majesty, I've been saving dis for... well, er... just such an occasion as dis!" he an-

nounced, grinning stupidly as he held out the cracked Cup. "May I present your Highness with dis Cup as a token of our gratitude for your timely victory over dem horrid Rats. It's not much I'm afraid, but I hope you'll like it."

"Well, thank you, O'Flattery." said the Queen. "I'm sure I will like it. It will look very pretty on my shelf at home, don't you think so?"

The Animals looked at O'Flattery and the Queen and burst out laughing.

Suddenly a tremendous din irrupted from the sky above.

They rushed to the top exit to look out. The sky was chaotic with feathers and noise. It was as if two huge cloud-giants, Snowstorm and Black Thunder, had clashed together in a titanic struggle for mastery of the sky. An aerial pitched battle raged between raucous crows, on the one hand, and screeching white gulls, on the other.

"I knew it," cried Sweeney in delight, "it's our pals, Pathos, Ethos and Erymos to de rescue!"

The Animals cheered.

"Dat should keep dem crows busy while we go to de Corbie Stone," said Sweeney.

"And what will you do when you get there?" A deep voice rumbled up the crevice, and a squat grey figure emerged from the lower depths. It was

Cranny.

"I am glad to see you," said Sweeney, "where's Nook?"

"He'll be along presently," said Cranny. "But what will you do when you get there?"

"Er, I t'ink what he's maybe trying to tell you," said O'Flattery, "is dat we should climb through de eye of de Corbie-stone right to de top."

"Eye? How do you know the stone's got an eye?" asked Cranny.

"Er, a little birdie told me," Sweeney muttered, shuffling uneasily.

"What sort of little birdie?" asked Cranny.

"Well, a big black pointy-beaked sort of birdie," squirmed Sweeney. "It told us how to find de Jewel when we was in de well, in exchange for…"

"The Cup! I see," said Mumbie.

"Well, well," said Cranny, "you may as well share the secret now, eh?"

"Yes. First, you climbs through de eye of de Corbie stone. Den you looks back down. And where de sun shines t'rough at midday, dat's where de Jewel is hid."

"Good. Now what time is it?" asked Cranny.

"Nearly midday," said Queen Mumbie, who always knew the position of the sun, so very important to bees.

"Hmm. Who's it to be?" asked Cranny gravely. "I'm too big to crawl through."

"I'll do it," said Pilgrim, "I'll fly up."

"No. That's too obvious. What we need is a cunning, crafty, sneaky sort of climber," said Cranny, looking in the general direction of O'Flattery.

"Who, me?" asked O'Flattery, for whom the direction of Cranny's glance was not general enough.

"B-b-but me eyesight's none too good," stammered O'Flattery in blind panic.

"Right. That's settled, then," said Cranny. "You'll climb, O'Flattery, and you, Pilgrim, will fly up to protect him. It will be very exposed on top of that bare rock."

O'Flattery felt ill. Exposed? His thoughts returned to Magpies and snake-pies. Before he could excuse himself on the grounds of a terrible attack of Indisposition coming on, which would render him quite incapable of being in dat position at the same time, Cranny pushed them forward.

The Animals bounded forth from the narrow defile, ran up the short slope to the ridge-top, and charged for the Rock.

The Corbie-stone looked huge at close range, a great flat mass of brimstone perched on its narrow pillar, a primeval sentinel standing impassively in the midst of the battle's din.

Crows scattered before their sudden onrush, but as they approached the Stone itself they found it surrounded by a ring of rats, commanded by King Ziggu himself from a low stone nearby.

"They must have found another way up," said Curd.

"We've got to get t'rough to dat Rock," said Sweeney.

"I'll deal with King Ziggu and his guard," said Cranny. "Curd and Sweeney, you've got to get O'Flattery through to the base of the rock and then fend off the rest of the rats."

"My subjects and I," said Queen Mumbie-Bumbee, "will provide low-flying air-cover. Have you all got your stings ready, Gels? Good. Ready for take off? Tally ho!"

"Charge!" cried Sweeney the Heenie.

They charged into the middle of the throng of rats. The rats bit and scratched like brambles, but were no match for Cranny and the bees that begirt him as he made directly for the King Rat.

Curd and Sweeney, with O'Flattery shielding his neck, ran on either side of him. Pilgrim flew just above and behind, ready to swoop down on any rats attacking from the sides.

Scratching and clawing, biting and barging, they forced back the rat-horde directly ahead of them until they reached the rock.

The rats closed ranks, surrounding the little band with a vast army, held at bay only by the fierce barbs of the bees.

O'Flattery slid off Sweeney's back onto the base of the rock and wriggled towards the overhang through which the hole ran.

Cranny cudgelled the Rat-King's bodyguard, forcing his way towards their leader.

Curd and Sweeney fought side-by-side, their backs against the rock, fending off wave after wave of rat attacks as O'Flattery climbed.

Far above the battle, Old Corbie, the Great Raven, soared, croaking his commands.

"Attack! Magpies, atta-CAAARCK!" he ordered, seeing his foes reach the Corbie Stone.

"Pike! A Pike! A Pike!" Stabbing and jabbing with pikes and beaks, Magpies screamed into the attack.

The first cohort of well-disciplined magpies drove Pilgrim from the Rock, and the second tore into the defenceless O'Flattery, spearing and pecking, trying to prize him from the rock.

O'Flattery inched his way up, as beak-blows tore dozens of holes in his tough cloth skin.

The Stone

Reaching the Eye of the Corbie-stone, he had a moment's respite from their attack as he wriggled through the hole in the rock.

Pilgrim Crow fought back furiously. He clawed his way to the top of the Rock, where he hovered over O'Flattery, emerging from the hole.

Even with Pilgrim Crow protecting his back as he reared up on the summit of the Stone to look back through the hole, O'Flattery felt as naked as a worm on a sun-baked road.

He could barely see for flying feathers. The sun's rays, passing through the eye of the rock, shone directly on an old dead birch tree behind the Corbie-stone.

In the centre of the patch of sunlight on the tree O'Flattery noticed a knot-hole where a branch must have been torn off the trunk in a storm. "Dat must be it! Dat must be de Great Raven's hidey-hole!" he yelled at the top of his voice, "It's in de branch-hole halfway up dat dead tree!"

Old Corbie, the Great Raven, seeing that the snake had dared climb atop his Rock without giving him his precious cracked Cup, swooped down like

a thunderbolt, knocking Pilgrim flying and hitting O'Flattery with such force that he nearly broke him in two. Grasping the poor snake in his strong talons like a hawk, the Raven carried him off into the sky.

As he rose higher and higher, O'Flattery watched his friends shrinking into the landscape below.

He could now see all the way to Birkwood, the river, and the Twins' home, his home…

"Traitor! Where's my Cup? Where's my precious Cup?" the Great Raven raved, "You promised me you'd get it from Queen Mumbie."

"I did, I did," cried O'Flattery.

"Where is it, then? I'll call off the attack if you give it to me. You can have your Brooch if only you get me my Cup back." The Great Raven looked down at the squirming snake. "Well?"

"Well, I gave it back, Sor. To Queen Mumbie-Bumbee, Sor," whimpered O'Flattery, "cos she rescued us from dem Rats, down in de rock dere."

"You buffoon! I sent the Rats to check you had the Cup and to escort you safely to my rock," cawed Old Corbie, the Great Raven, "but Queen Mumbie and her bees attacked them first. She only came looking for the Cup, and you gave it to her."

"But we t'ought dem Bees was

coming to our rescue. Dem Rats attacked us in de barn only dis morning, so dey did!"

"On my orders. I knew Queen Mumbie would come after it. Die, traitor, CRAAA!" With that loud cry, the Raven dropped him. O'Flattery plummeted down, wriggling helplessly in the air. Slowly at first the ground rose towards him, then faster and faster...

A jolt broke his fall, and he looked up to see a black ragged canopy flapping about him: it was Pilgrim! Tumbling together, Pilgrim tried desperately to recover his flight.

"O, Pilgrim, t'ank goodness..." cried O'Flattery.

"O'Flattery, I... can't..." Pilgrim lost his grip, and had to watch helplessly as the hapless snake crashed onto the rocks below.

"Curd, Sweeney! To the tree!" shouted Cranny, beating his way through the rat-mass like a thresher through a field of wheat.

Curd and Sweeney dashed in behind Cranny's great bulk to reach the old birch tree, fending off attacks by the rats and magpies.

"Climb, Curd, climb," shouted Cranny, as he and Sweeney, backs to the trunk, faced the onrushing rats.

"Capture the tree at all costs!" screamed King Ziggu, infuriated by the stalwart resistance of so small a band against his hordes. But as fast as they came on, the stinging barbs of Queen Mumbie-Bumbee's bee-swarm drove the rats over a cliff that fell away to one side of the dead tree.

Great King Ziggu himself charged with his bodyguard of giant battle-hardened rats, slavering and squealing, flailing cudgel-blows in berserk frenzy, forcing Cranny and Sweeney to give ground...

Curd began to climb, desperate to reach the knot-hole where the Brooch was hidden. The old windswept birch leaned backwards, making the climb easy but for the mobbing magpies. He hugged the trunk, gripping the rough bark with his claws as the vicious birds tried to prize him off.

Pilgrim Crow, abandoning all hope for poor O'Flattery, tore into the mobbing magpies with a fury, giving Curd a breathing space to climb the last few feet to the hole.

From his vantage point high in the sky, Old Corbie the Raven saw Curd on his tree. His Secret was out! His Hidey discovered and he himself betrayed by the traitors with whom he had made a deal to recover his stolen Cup.

"Crook! CROOK!" he cried in anguish.

In the great aerial battle that raged that afternoon over the Brimstone Ridge the gulls were now in the ascendancy as they swooped, tumbled and soared in pursuit of his ragged corvid cohorts.

All seemed lost.

"I'll turn the tables yet on those crooks," Old Corbie cried, "Krok-krok-krok!"

He tilted his head skywards, and with a loud "KONK!" he rolled over onto his back in mid-air.

Like an explosion all the birds in the air, gulls and crows, scattered to the four winds, fleeing the falcon they thought was about to dive into their midst to snatch a victim.

The great Trickster, Old Corbie, was left gliding in an empty sky.

The sudden flight of the magpies left Curd free to search for the Brooch. He looked into the hole in the trunk. At first he could see nothing: his head was blocking out the light. Cocking his head to one side, he peered in

with one eye, as if around a corner. Suddenly a little eye glinted back at him out of the hole. There was something there, and just within reach. Stretching in as far as he could with his paw, he fumbled about. Something caught on his claws, and he swiftly hooked it out.

It was the Brooch, object of their Great Adventure: Mum's own precious Emerald and Diamond Brooch!

"I have it!" Curd yelled exultantly, holding it up for all to see. It shone magnificently in the bright sunlight. Gripping his prize between his teeth, Curd started down the tree.

THWUMP! The first bolt struck him! The Raven dug his claws into his fur to tear him bodily from the tree. Curd clung on for dear life.

CRUMP! A second bolt jarred the dead tree to its

roots.

So intent on Curd was Old Corbie that he never saw the heron that struck him. Both Curd and the Raven were knocked out of the tree; Curd falling with such a thump that the wind was knocked out of him, and the Brooch with it.

Old Corbie grasped the great grey bird in his talons as he fell and the pair of them, locked together, tumbled over the cliff.

Seeing the magpies flee and the fall of the Great Raven, King Ziggu looked about him for a line of retreat.

Cranny, seizing his chance to rid himself once and for all of this loathsome pest, bore down on the obnoxious Rat-king, driving him to the very edge of the cliff over which so many of his followers had met their doom.

Cursing and screaming, King Ziggu fought as fiercely as any corned rat until finally Queen Mumbie herself darted in and stabbed the rat on his sensitive snout with her fiery sting.

Blinded with pain, the Rat King staggered, tripped and tumbled down the rock-face, never to be seen again.

Seeing their invincible leader perish, the panic-stricken rats fell into disorderly flight. They scrambled over and fought each other in their haste to escape.

As the last of the rats scampered down the slopes for home, Curd and his friends paused to

recover their breath and count the cost.

"Poor O'Flattery is dead," croaked Pilgrim Crow.

"He can't be!" cried Sweeney. "He's too crafty to fall for a trick like getting killed."

"He is," insisted Pilgrim. "I couldn't save him when the Great Raven dropped him. He was dashed on the rocks at the foot of the cliff."

Sweeney sat down in disbelief.

Had not O'Flattery been the most companionable scarf a fellow could wish to wear? Had not he, Sweeney the Heenie, great warrior and Champion of the Plain Man, carried him too far, through too many adventures, for an end such as this? For what? For a silly Adventure to capture a stupid Brooch. O'Flattery deserved better. He at least deserved a Memorial for his bravery, a Headstone for his grave. And what better than a jewelled headstone?

"De Brooch!" yelled Sweeney, leaping up and advancing on Curd. "Gimme dat Brooch!"

"Calm down," urged Pilgrim.

"Calm down nuttin!" Sweeney growled. "O'Flattery died for dat Brooch, and he's going to have it! It's going to be his Memorial – his gravestone."

"But it's our Mum's Brooch!" protested Curd,"What about the Twins' Birthday? If we don't get it home by tomorrow Mum's going to get rid of us all, and we'll never see each other again."

"I don't care!" shouted Sweeney, "I've lost O'Flattery forever already. Why should I care anymore?"

"Because we do," said Pilgrim, "care for you, that is. We've still got each other, haven't we?"

"But I t'ought..." began Sweeney, "I t'ought we was... "

"Rivals?" Pilgrim replied, "no, only in fun. Really, we're friends."

"Yes," added Curd, "what would we do without you and O'oooF..."

Pilgrim gave Curd a sharp jab in the ribs.

"...I mean, your fun and games?" spluttered Curd.

"Give it to him," said Cranny to Curd, "if he wants it that badly."

"Oh! I haven't got it!" cried Curd, suddenly realizing that he hadn't.

CHAPTER EIGHTEEN.   **The Setting.**

"Don't be silly, Curd. Of course you have it," said Pilgrim.

"You're hiding it!" snapped Sweeney.

"I'm not. I must have dropped it near the tree when I fell," insisted Curd.

He ran to the tree and started searching at its foot.

The others joined him, and soon all were bent low, scouring the ground around, under every rock, in every crevice and bush, hunting for the missing Brooch.

"Bottoms up, lads!"

At this familiar voice all looked round.

It was O'Flattery, wrapped around the long neck of the Heron. Both were safe, and their old friend O'Flattery looked not much the worse for wear.

"O'Flattery!" cried Sweeney, "we all t'ought you was dead!"

"Well, as it happened, I landed in a t'ick clump of heather down dere. Next t'ing I knew, everyting went black. And flatten me if wasn't hisself, Old Corbie, landed right on top o' me, together wid yer man here, Mr. Heron." O'Flattery laughed, "and what did dey do but fight and scrabble all over me? I thought to meself: I've had me fill o' dis! So I sunk me fangs hard into Corbie's heel, and de old fella just goes and keels over in a dead faint!"

"O'Flattery!" shouted Sweeney as he ran over to him.

O'Flattery wrapped himself snugly round his old friend's neck. The animals crowded round, praising and patting him.

"Let's be finding dis Brooch, then," said O'Flattery, to draw attention away from himself.

"Oh, the Brooch!" exclaimed Curd.

"Come on. We'd better hurry if we're to find it before it gets dark. The sun is setting," said Pilgrim, turning to go back to the tree, "and tomorrow is the Twin's Birthday, so we've got to find it now."

The Animals looked at him, but no one followed.

"Stop gawking!" said Pilgrim stuffily, "I'm not going to find it all by myself"

The Animals giggled.

"You couldn't really," laughed Curd, "seeing as how it's on your back."

Sweeney plucked the jewelled Brooch from the feathers in which it had lodged when it shot from Curd's mouth when he fell.

The Animals roared with laughter. Curd turned to Cranny and pressed his paw into his hand: "Thank you for all your help."

"That's alright, we did the best we could," replied Cranny.

"Talking of WE," said Sweeney, "whatever happened to Nook?"

"Here I am."

The Animals turned to see the Heron transforming slowly before their eyes into Nook, the lean and lanky mine-goblin, so familiar to Sweeney and O'Flattery.

"T'was you all de time!" exclaimed Sweeney.

"Thank you for coming to my rescue, twice!" said Curd, "as Heron, I mean."

"Alright, alright," croaked Pilgrim, "it's time we were going. It's getting

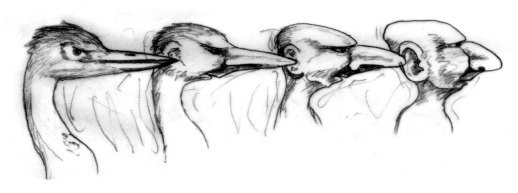

late, and we've a long march ahead of us."

"Don't worry about that," said Nook, "we've arranged transport, and here it comes."

The cry of gulls announced the arrival of Ethos, Pathos and Erymos, with the great Balloonafuss in tow.

They alighted on the top of the Corbie Stone and secured the bulging Balloonafuss to the rock…

"Damn if I'm going to get my lines snagged among those wicked rocks down there," roared the Fuss. "You'll have to climb on up and hop in."

One by one, the Animals climbed up through the Corbie's eye to the top, except Pilgrim.

First Curd clawed his way tightly through the hole. Then Sweeney and O'Flattery.

O'Flattery wriggled through and then Sweeney stretched up for a hand because hyenas don't have climbing claws like lions: they prefer digging. Curd grabbed his front paws and pulled him up. It was a bit tight around Sweeney's tummy, so Pilgrim too pulled and Nook, who was taller, pushed from below.

POP! He shot into the air like a cork from a bottle into the great soft head of the Balloonafuss.

"Oomph! What de…" Sweeney dropped with a plop into the basket.

The basket got a nasty wobble on, and all hands were needed to steady it.

"I say, that was a bit over the top," grumped the Fuss, as the rest of the crew clambered aboard.

"Off you go, now," shouted Nook from below, "and so must we, goodbye!" He winked at Cranny, and the pair of them set off along the ridge as the balloon and its occupants slowly rose into the air.

"Isn't it high," gasped Curd, as he looked at the sheer drop to the ground over the Corbie Stone's beak as they edged away from the Rock.

"Dat's nothing," boasted O'Flattery, who had been much higher himself. "Just wait till you get up dere!" He nodded nonchalantly towards the sky.

"Look, dere's Nook and Cranny," cried Sweeney, pointing along the ridge.

"Where?" asked Pilgrim? "I can't see them."

"Neither can I," said Curd.

"I can," whispered O'Flattery in Sweeney's ear. He had recognised Nook and Cranny's unmistakable craggy features set in stone on the ridge, not far away. So, Nook and Cranny were themselves the very Landscape of which they were the Guardians! "Look see, Curd, just along dat top ridge."

"Oh, yes, now I can see them," said Curd.

The Balloonafuss rose majestically into the sunset, towed west by the three gulls, and followed by a dark cloud of bees.

"Goodbye Nook; goodbye Cranny!" they all shouted, as the rocks fell away below them and receded into the darkening landscape.

Curd the Lion took a long last glance towards the ridge of Brimstone and the Corbie-stone itself, glowing in the light of the setting sun.

"Look! The Corbie-stone's on fire!" he shouted.

The top of the rock seemed aflame with reddened clouds behind it. The

Animals could make out a form just like that of the Great Black Raven stretching its wings wide as flames engulfed its dark silhouette in their brightness.

A dark wispy cloud rose above the rocky horizon against the pink glow of the reflected sunset. The cloud strangely assumed the shape of the Great Raven flying across the evening sky.

"A Phoenix!" cried Sweeney, hoarsely, "a Phoenix!"

"Don't be silly, that's just a Roc!" said Pilgrim, who had seen one once in the Twin's Book of Myth and Legend.

Slowly the cloud drifted away to become lost in the darkening sky as the sun sank into the western horizon.

Below them the stream threaded its silver way through the darkness, guiding them in its meandering way towards their home. As the Balloonafuss descended slowly, the Animals could make out the lights of the hamlet, where Henry, Henrietta and all the family lived, winking through the trees.

Queen Mumbie-bumbee and all her subjects accompanied them all the way to Birkwood. As they left, Pilgrim said: "You will, your Majesty, permit us to visit you, won't you?"

"Of course, of course, my dear, dear friends," replied the Queen, "you will always find a welcome in my realm." With that Queen Mumbie and her bumblebees departed to their earthen home with her precious Cup.

It was late as they approached the hamlet and no one saw the ghostly Balloonafuss make its silent descent as the three gulls steered it into the Twin's garden, across the road from their house.

The basket landed with a thud, and was dragged along the grass for a few yards, spilling its occupants, before the gulls could bring it to a halt.

As they got to their feet, Curd turned to the great Fuss, "Thank you, Mr. Balloonafuss."

"Professor," hissed the Balloonafuss, a little deflated by this lack of formality. "I have to be off now. I have the whole wide World to think of, you know. Time and tide wait for no moon."

With a mighty roar of his burner, he puffed himself up to his full dignity and ascended rapidly into the darkness until he was just a moon in the sky.

Pathos, Ethos, and Erymos, the three seagulls, made their farewells. "I guess we showed those crows they can't go round bullying us anymore, eh?"

"We certainly did!"

Sweeney shouted after them, as they flew away to their colony.

For a moment the Animals could see the three gulls silhouetted against the moon, then they were gone.

Curd the Lion, Pilgrim Crow, Sweeney the Heenie and O'Flattery the Snake turned and walked in silence towards the tunnel under the lane that led to Henry and Henrietta's house; a tunnel who's gloomy arches held no mystery in the dark now, after so many adventures.

The lounge window was open. They could hear Mum clanking about in the kitchen. They scrambled onto the low sill of the open window and dropped to the floor. Henry's Uncle was puffing on a cigar in the big leather armchair.

"Quick," whispered Pilgrim, "let's sneak upstairs to the Twins' room, before Mum comes back to shut the window."

Across the living-room carpet, under the smoke-haze that hung three feet from the floor they crept past the armchair.

"Aark!" Pilgrim squawked with pain and hopped up and down, holding his foot.

"Shhh!" whispered Curd.

"There's something in my foot," protested Pilgrim, hopping mad.

Curd looked. It was a pine needle, embedded in the sole of his foot. He took it in his teeth and pulled.

"There! Fancy, after all we've been through." said Curd.

"Hurry," said Sweeney impatiently.

The Animals followed the smoke trail as it curled up the stairs.

Curd sneezed. Uncle's fondness for cigars was, Mum's fondness for her brother notwithstanding, the main reason for the rarity of his visits.

Reaching Henry and Henrietta's room, they found the door open, just a crack, as usual. They pushed it wider and crept in. Retiring into a corner behind a cupboard, they curled up together.

"Well, we made it," whispered Curd the Lion. "We got the Brooch back in time and saved the Twins."

He clutched the Brooch that had precipitated them into such Adventures as the Twins had never dreamed of.

"Yes, we did," agreed Pilgrim Crow.

"If only," whispered Curd, as he snuggled back down, "if only the Twins could know... about our Great Adventure, I mean."

"Maybe dey will," muttered Sweeney the Heenie, "maybe dey will at dat."

The animals dropped off, one by one, snug in the safety of the Twins' room, dreaming each of their various exploits and in the quiet of the night the house returned to normal.

It was while tidying the bedroom the next morning that Henry's and Henrietta's mother discovered the torn, muddy, bedraggled heap of Animals in the corner behind the wardrobe.

Henrietta was playing innocently with Ballad the dog in the lounge, watched over by her Uncle, quietly puffing his breakfast cigar and smiling to himself in that way smokers do.

Henry, idly kicking a football about, was thinking: "What's Uncle so pleased with himself about?"

"Henry! HENRIETTA!"

The siren-call burst through the smoke like a fire-engine.

"You'd better go, children," said Uncle, "I think she wants you."

Henry, followed by Henrietta, went running upstairs to their bedroom, where Mother was waiting.

"What on earth have you been doing with these toys?" she asked, severely.

"Nothing," answered Henrietta.

"Nothing," answered Henry.

"And what is my jewelled brooch doing here?" she asked.

"I don't know," replied Henry and Henrietta together.

"Perhaps it walked," added Henry, looking at Henrietta with a smirk.

"Perhaps it got caught in Curd's fur?" said Henrietta, frowning at her brother.

Fury twitched in Mother's eyebrows. Then it fell off and her expression softened: "Well, anyway, we've got it back now. And that's what matters, isn't it?"

"Yes," said Henry and Henrietta together. They smiled at Mother, then at each other. They chuckled at each other's smiles, then giggled, then roared with laughter as Mother finally gave in and smiled too.

"But be more careful in future, please, Twins," she laughed

"We will," they both shouted, together, a bit too loud.

The Twins' mother stitched up Sweeney's torn ears, and all the other rips and tears in their Animals. She washed them all thoroughly and hung them, dripping, on the washing line to dry in the cold breeze of that sunny winter's morning.

And of course Henry and Henrietta did get their presents on their birthday, that day.

Afterward.   **The Book.**

Henry's and Henrietta's Father was always busy. He never had enough time. It wasn't that he didn't care, but he was shorter than the Twins' mother and Curd figured that that might have something to do with it.

When he wasn't too busy, he was too tired to play. He did, however, often take the Twins and their Animals out of harm's way to visit Grandpa up on the Hill.

Grandpa lived on a farm near the ridge and often took care of the Twins and their Animals during the holidays. They were fond of playing on the rocks of Brimstone, especially in the summer when it was hot.

They went up there whenever they could and the three of them had many a fine picnic on the rocks. The Twins' father would bring them up to the farm in the mornings, and Grandpa would walk them back home in the evenings.

Grandpa was a great storyteller. On their picnics they would sit the Animals around in a circle to listen to these wonderful tales.

One day the Twins left the Animals behind at the farm when the strap of Henry's rucksack broke, and there they stayed until Grandpa fixed it. To pass the time the Animals told him of their Great Adventure.

After they had all gone home, Grandpa sat down in the long summer evenings and wrote it all down. He drew pictures of their Animals, and of all the creatures they met, then bound the book in an old leather book-cover.

The next time Henry and Henrietta came for the day, Grandpa took them to the Corbie Stone, and together they climbed the rock.

Henry and Henrietta arranged their Animals in a circle; sitting one in each of the hollow cups in the rock and then sat down beside Grandpa.

As they looked out across the valley, hazy in the summer sunshine, Grandpa said: "Today is a very special day."

"Why is it a special day, Grandpa?" asked Henry.

155

Afterward

"Today is the day on which I am going to tell you the story of your Animals."

And he did.

"Did all that really happen to our Animals?" asked Henrietta, as the Twins, their Animals and Grandpa climbed down from the Corbie Stone.

"Yes it did. And this is for you both to take care of," replied Grandpa, handing her the book, "so that you do not forget."

"Grandpa?" said Henry, "in your drawings – did you really mean for Nook to look a bit like Uncle…"

"…and for Cranny to look a bit like you," added Henrietta, "except that he has no hair at all?"

"Do they?" chuckled Grandpa, opening up the book again. "Now you mention it I suppose there is a bit of a similarity. What a coincidence. It must be my lack of imagination. We often draw things we are familiar with without realising."

As they wandered down the steep stony lane to their own house, Henrietta clutched the leather-bound book tightly to her breast. In Henry's mended rucksack, the Animals chattered along behind about their Amazing Adventure in the Land at the Back of Beyond.

Dear reader,

Do you remember Queen Mumbie-Bumbee and her six poster bed with its wonderfully embroidered pillowcase depicting Subjects of all sorts: flowers, trees, birds, animals and bees, wonderfully intermingled to suggest all manner of stories? And how, when you fell asleep on it, you found yourself in the Land of Nod?

Well, that's where they go in the next story. What adventures they will have there, and what stories they will have to tell of that magical Land!

Against all advice from my editors, I am going to tell, not show, you a little bit about the Secret of getting there, so if you want to know more, read on...

To the first person giving the right answer to the MinorBore's Great Riddle after it is published – not any old answer, but THE answer (and I'll bet no one can in a year and a day) – I will give four original illustrations from this book, and that will be a nice surprise. Surprise? Well, that's my secret.

BOOK TWO

The Ineffable Emperor

or,
Curd's travels to the Land of Nod
in the Great Sea of Slumber,
and of all that happened there.

CHAPTER ONE.   **Ill beginnings.**

On Friday Henrietta fell ill. She took to her bed. At first they thought it was the fish. Not that she'd had any. They thought it was the prospect of fish.

Mum cooked fish every Friday, because she had Religion and with that you get a smelly house once a week on Fridays.

But it wasn't that. Teatime came and went and she didn't get better, which she would have done if it had been that.

She even lost interest in her toys. It didn't seem to matter what tricks Sweeney the Heenie and O'Flattery the Snake played, she just looked blankly through them. They couldn't understand it one bit. It was almost as if they didn't exist!

She sank into a state of Lassitude (it's a thing girls get quite often when they lose all interest in anything and just want to lie down for a while. This is quite different to the Laditude that boys get when they just can't rise up in the morning from the Longitudinal position in bed till after half past eleven at the earliest).

The family were worried. But Dad said, "It'll all look different in the morning," which cheered them all up.

And it did. In the morning Henry didn't want to wake up. This could have been Laditude but for the fact that he looked a little green about the gills, like someone who was about to be sick.

Neither of them could eat any breakfast, not even their Saturday morning bacon and eggs, which was unheard of. Nor lunch. On Saturday afternoon the doctor was called in.

He listened and felt, he prodded and probed;
He searched for symptoms like a miner for gold.
He hit them with hammers on elbows and knees.
He tickled their feet and gave them a squeeze.

"With no swellings or lumps, it's not Measles or Mumps,
And certainly not Pneumonia.
And though they won't move, I just cannot prove
It is Impudent Catatonia!"

"I can't say for sure, but I think I've a Cure,
For whatever-it-is that ails them.
Just give them these pills, my "Cure-for-all-Ills",
And it'll wipe out the Bug that assails them."

And, after all that fuss and bother, he left, leaving a mess of long words behind him for Mum to clear up.

On Sunday, Grandpa came down from his Hill to pay them a visit. He had heard from the Gossips in the village that the young Twins were poorly.
" Well, well, well," he said, which they weren't of course. "What's all this then? What's all this fuss about you two being poorly, eh?"
Henry and Henrietta just looked at him and didn't even have the energy to say Hello.
"Dear me, this must be serious," said Grandpa, sitting on Henrietta's bed and stroking her hair. "Tell me what's the matter."
"I don't know," they both said at once. "We just feel sick and can't move," they said.
"I'll tell you what. Why don't you both sit next to me and I'll read you a chapter or two from 'The Amazing Adventures of Curd the Lion (and Us!) in the Land at the Back of Beyond,' eh? How about that?"
"Ok," they said, as if they didn't care a bit. But they did. And soon he was reading and talking with all the voices and it was just as if Curd and his friends had come to life.
"Wait a minute," said Henry. "We'll just get them so they can sit with us," continued Henrietta, because they both thought alike so that each

knew what the other was going to say.

Soon there were seven of them: Grandpa in the middle with the book, Henry on his right with Curd the Lion and Pilgrim Crow, Henrietta on his left with Sweeney the Heenie and O'Flattery the Snake.

Very soon after that they were into the Adventure and had forgotten their poorliness and were chuckling and even laughing now and then.

Eventually Grandpa closed the book and said, "That's better. You look much better already. I must stop now, so you can get some rest. And I'll come and see how you are tomorrow. I promise."

The next morning when Mum looked in to open the curtains, the Twins seemed to be just as bad as the day before. But when Grandpa called in to read to them that evening, they seemed to perk up a bit.

This went on for several days. Up and down each day, showing no real signs of getting better. Mum and Dad began to despair.

And so did Henry's and Henrietta's Animals. Until suddenly…

" I think I know what it is," announced Pilgrim Crow. "I think I know why Henry and Henrietta are ill."

"What is it?" cried all the Animals.

"They are pining for an Adventure," he announced grandly.

The silence that followed lasted for as long as the Animals thought about this, and that took quite a long time. It was only interrupted when Curd, who often thought shorter, or less, than the others asked: "What do you mean, pining for an Adventure?"

"Well, it's obvious," said Pilgrim, "It's only when Grandpa reads the story of Our Great Adventure that they cheer up, isn't it?"

"Yes."

"And it's only since Grandpa wrote down the story of Our Great Adventure and gave it to them that they became ill like this, right?"

"Right."

"Yes, but how does that make them ill?" asked Curd.

"Well, obviously, they want to have an Adventure like Ours. But they don't know how. So they're pining away with worry and such," continued Pilgrim Crow.

"Den we must find one for dem, mustn't we?" cried Sweeney the Heenie eagerly.

"Dat's easy to say," retorted O'Flattery, "but how?"

" I don't know," answered Pilgrim, "but one thing's for sure. If we don't find a way, then they might pine away into nothing."

"And that wouldn't be so good, would it?" said Curd.

"No, that would be bad," added Pilgrim.

"Very bad," they all chorused.

A long silence followed while they all thought.

An even longer silence followed that while they all thought again.

"I've got an idea," said Pilgrim.

"That's good," said Curd.

"How do you know? He hasn't even said it yet," hissed O'Flattery.

"I'll go and see Queen Mumbie-Bumbee," said Pilgrim.

"Dat's it?" snorted O'Flattery, "Dat's your idea? Huh."

"Why Queen Mumbie?" asked Curd.

"Because she's bound to know a remedy, with all her medicines and stuff," said Pilgrim.

"Perhaps you could get some magic honey-cakes," said Sweeney the Heenie.

"Better still, some mumble-mead," said Curd, "that cheered me up."

"And me."

"Me too."

"That's settled, then. I, Pilgrim Crow, will fly poste-haste without delay or further ado directly to the old hawthorn in Birkwood and pay a visit to Queen Mumbie-Bumbee herself," concluded Pilgrim.

"He's so clever, isn't he?" whispered Curd.

"Dat's because he's got Wisdom," replied Sweeney.

"Like what he keeps under his hat, you mean?" asked Curd.

"Something like dat," replied O'Flattery.

"Does that mean Sir Rush has Wisdom too?" asked Curd, thinking of his bald shiny pate.

"Probably," replied Sweeney, wondering when this would end.

"Then why doesn't Pilgrim go visit Sir Rush?" asked Curd.

"Queen Mumbie's closer," interrupted Pilgrim, who had overheard this whispered dialogue. "And we're in a hurry, aren't we?" said Pilgrim firmly, "Any more questions before I go?"

"No," they all replied quickly to help him along.

"Er, Pilgrim," said Curd, as Pilgrim Crow flapped his wings and rose into the air and hovered for a moment.

"What?" croaked Pilgrim testily as he swept towards the bedroom window.

"The window's shut!" exclaimed Curd. Pilgrim dropped to the floor with a thud.

"Who shud the widdow?" demanded Pilgrim angrily as he pulled on the end of his beak to straighten it out again. "Who shuddit? It was oped last tibe I looked."

"I think Mum did," suggested Curd, "I heard Henry complaining he was cold."

"Well you might have told me," said Pilgrim, dusting himself down. "Doesn't she know that fresh air is the best thing for good health. No wonder they're ill, cooped up like this."

"You could try de bathroom window," suggested Sweeney the Heenie, "dat one's always open."

"On account'o de pong," chuckled O'Flattery.

Pilgrim flew away to investigate this claim without another word.

"I think he's annoyed," whispered Curd, "I tried to warn him."

"Important Animals like him don't often listen," replied Sweeney.

A moment later a black shadow flitted across the group and they looked up to see Pilgrim hovering outside the window before heading East towards Birkwood.

"All we can do is wait, now," said Curd.

"I hope he brings back some honey-cakes," said Sweeney, licking his lips.

"I hope he brings back some mumble-mead," said O'Flattery.

"If he does, they're not for you," said Curd.

"Nor you, neither," retorted O'Flattery.

"Shush, you'll upset Henry and Henrietta, if you shout," pleaded Sweeney.

"Hmph!" The Animals glowered at each other and went their separate ways. They weren't really angry with each other so much as angry at not being able to help poor Henry and Henrietta.

CHAPTER TWO.   **As the crow flies.**

Pilgrim Crow flew up the mill-stream until he reached Mother Beanie's bridge, then veered left and over Birkwood until he reached the ancient hawthorn tree that marked Queen Mumbie-Bumbee's house.

He rapped loudly on her heavy wooden front door and waited, pacing up and down with his hands behind his back. He was on urgent business, you see, and that required the right degree of seriousness, and that required a certain amount of practice.

He had just decided that a bit of forward tilt, together with looking down at the ground about four feet ahead and frowning heavily, gave him just the right air of gravity when there was a clicking and scuffling at the door, and the door opened a little and a bee's head poked itself through the gap.

"Yes, what is it?" the bee asked rudely, "Have you got an Invitation?"

"Invitation?" replied Pilgrim.

"Yes, Invitation," said the bumptious bee. "Entry only by Appointment to her Majesty Queen Mumbie-Bumbee. Have you got a Royal Appointment?"

The door was ajar and Pilgrim could see the label now, just below the Royal Coat-of-Arms: "By Appointment to her Majesty Queen Mumbie-Bumbee," just like on the honey-jars they had at home, because the Twins mother only bought the best.

"Well yes, I have, actually," said Pilgrim, "Queen Mumbie herself invited

164

me to come back any time last time we were here."

"The last time?" said the doorkeeper bee, "I've never seen you before in my life."

"You weren't here then," replied Pilgrim, "It was before your time."

"She'd have forgotten, then, likely. Where's your Card?"

"I haven't got a Card. I told you, it was a personal invitation."

"No Card, no appointment. That's the rules." The bee-guard was beginning to enjoy this.

"No, no Card, of course not," Pilgrim was getting hot under the collar.

"Well, if you care to leave your name, I'll go and see if her Majesty will see you," the bee smirked and slammed the door shut. (Bees do smirk, quite a lot, though it's very difficult to see, because they are very sure of their own superiority, what with having such a complex civilisation and full employment, childcare and such laid on, so that the women can work all day long, leaving the men to lounge about all day and drone on about their prowess and what they will do one day.)

Pilgrim hammered angrily on the door. Suddenly a little peep-hole opened in the middle of the door and the same bee peered out, "Yes?" (You may wonder how Pilgrim knew it was the same bee, since they all look alike, but he knew. It was a matter of manners.)

"Let me in," demanded Pilgrim.

"Name please," demanded the bee back.

"I told you: Pilgrim Crow, Curd the Lion's friend," snapped Pilgrim.

"Business?"

"None of yours..." started Pilgrim, but, realising he wasn't going to get anywhere with this obtuse bee, he continued, "I'm on an important mission to save Henry and Henrietta and I need her Majesty's advice."

"Advice?" said the bee, "well why didn't you say so? She's always ready to advise, she is so wise, you know. A moment please." The little door-within-a-door slammed shut with a click and Pilgrim found himself alone once more.

A couple of minutes later, the door swung open and the bee footman stood aside, bowing courteously low.

Pilgrim stepped inside and walked straight to Queen Mumbie's Hall, because he knew the way already. Pairs of guards uncrossed their halberds to let him pass.

"What a change from the last time," thought Pilgrim, "when there was no one here but Mumbie herself. It's a bit like a Royal Palace now."

Which of course it was. In her Royal Chamber Queen Mumbie received him warmly.

"How are you, dear Pilgrim? How are Curd, Sweeney and that snake,

O'Flattery, is it? And what brings you here? Advice, I hear."

"Oh, we're all fine, your Majesty," answered Pilgrim, "and we do need advice. You see Henry and Henrietta, whose toys we are…"

"Toys? I don't quite follow," said the Queen.

"Well, like your subjects, I suppose," explained Pilgrim.

"So they're Royal then, are they, Henry and Henrietta, like me?"

"I suppose so, yes, in a way you could say that," said Pilgrim, "Henry and Henrietta are both very ill. And nothing the doctors do makes them better. We're all very worried, so see…"

"I see," said the Queen, "then we must help them. Describe their symptoms. How do they look? Have they got a temperature? Are they aching anywhere?"

Pilgrim Crow described as best he could all the things that were wrong with the Twins.

At one point Queen Mumbie-Bumbee interrupted him and asked: "And are they down the dumps. A little green about the gills, perhaps?"

"Yes," replied Pilgrim.

"And do they not play with you as much as you would like, anymore?"

"No they don't much," said Pilgrim, wondering how she could possibly know.

"And do they," the Queen asked, "do they, when you look at them or talk to them, do they perhaps look sideways?"

"How do you know?" he asked out loud, "Yes, they do."

"And could it be said," continued the Queen, "could it be said (she liked to repeat herself for effect; she had studied law once upon a time) that they seem to be IGNORING you?"

"Well, yes, I suppose you could say that," said Pilgrim, hating to admit it.

"I did. But can you?" insisted the Queen.

"Er, yes," said Pilgrim.

"Then I have it!" chortled the Queen, "Tea?"

"Yes please," said Pilgrim.

Queen Mumbie clapped her hands: "A cup of tea for my guest." Her servants scuttled out to do her bidding.

"What we have here," announced the Queen grandly, "is a textbook case of Jealousy, pure and simple!"

"Jealousy, your Majesty?"

"Yes. Jealousy. They are jealous of the Grand Adventure you had because they weren't on it. And they are Pining Away for an Adventure, just like yours," she added, and nodded in appreciation of the loud clapping of her subjects at this latest example of her Imperial Wisdom.

"Enough, enough," she said, gently waving a small handkerchief to subdue the applause. She turned to Pilgrim and whispered confidentially from behind her kerchief. "They do so adore me. I'm like a Mother to them all, you know."

Pining for an Adventure? Pilgrim thought to himself. But that's what I said. How could she know? Can she read my thoughts? He felt his head and looked in the mirror to see if his brain had leaked. Maybe she had said it because it was true and they were both right. He felt better immediately, and not the least bit jealous that she had got all the credit for his idea.

"And an Adventure they must have, if they are to recover, you know," announced the Queen.

"But how? How can they have an Adventure if they are both so ill?" asked Pilgrim Crow.

"There's only one way," said Queen Mumbie-Bumbee. "They mustn't know they are having it until they are in it."

"How?"

"The Land of Nod," she announced, triumphantly. "They must go to the Land of Nod. And you, Pilgrim Crow, must find the Key to the Door to the Land of Nod, if they are to get there."

"But how? Where do I look?" asked Pilgrim.

"There is a strange bird," said the Queen, "and he goes by the name of 'Dodongs'."

"Dodongs?" Pilgrim interrupted, "I've met him already once, on our last Adventure. He's a two-headed..."

"Dodo?" interrupted the Queen back. "But you must never call him that. Not if you want his help. As I was saying, the Dodongs is the Key. You must persuade him to give you two of his magic feathers."

"But he doesn't have any feathers. He has scales of armour instead. So he can't fly." Said Pilgrim.

"Oh, but he can! Not in your world, mind, but in the Land of Nod you never saw a more graceful flier," said the Queen dreamily. "But to get back to the case in hand. You may know his heads are called Nid and Nod. Well, when they listen to a story they like they start to nod their heads. So you must tell them a story, and once you've got their heads nodding nicely, you must turn it into a very sad story."

"Why a very sad story?" asked Pilgrim.

"Because, my dear," answered the Queen, "come closer, dear. This is a Secret," she whispered, "they keep their feathers hidden on the inside. So, you must do as I did, when I got some of their feathers. I told them such a sad story that they couldn't help themselves, they sighed and sighed until they were dizzy with sadness, until each head nodded up and sighed Down. And before they knew it, I had two of their feathers, which I have to this day."

"But if you've got two, couldn't I borrow those?" asked Pilgrim, "I would give them back."

"Impossible!" snapped the Queen, rising to her feet. Seeing the alarm on Pilgrim's face, she mellowed, and added, "it's impossible, you see, once you have them, to give them up. Not to anybody. Not for anything. They're too precious. Like my Cup. I'm afraid you will have to find your own."

"If I can find the Dodongs and if I can persuade him to sigh out two feathers. What then?" asked Pilgrim.

"Then you must put one inside Henry's pillow and one inside Henrietta's pillow and all gather round and wait. The magic feathers will, once they are sound asleep, transport them to the Land of Nod. So you must be close by if you're going to be ready to go with them."

"But how will we know when they are going to be transported to the Land of Nod?" asked Pilgrim.

"Watch their mouths," replied the Queen. "When they roll onto their backs and their mouths open a bit: watch carefully. Suddenly, you will hear a noise…"

"Oh, snoring, you mean," said Pilgrim.

"Yes, and that announces their departure," said Queen Mumbie.
"Watch closely, or you'll miss it. A little wispy curl of breath will emerge ever so slightly from their mouths and this will be their Pixie-selves creeping out. It's easier to see on a cold, cold night…"

"Yes, I've seen it! I've seen it!" cried Pilgrim Crow, "But I didn't know that's what it was."

"Not many do. And they're off like a shot, unless you catch them," said the Queen. "As soon as you see them, you must whisper softly: 'Pixie, pixie, ever-so tricksie; become thee light as I can see thee!' And they will come out of their vapour cloud and become visible to you. Then you must name them quickly before they can turn again to mist."

"But what will we name them?" asked Pilgrim.

"Pixie-Henry and Pixie-Henrietta, of course," said the wise Queen, "but then again, that's a bit long for an Adventure. I know, you must call them Pee-Hee and Pee-Ha for short. Then they will be able to find their way back again to your own Henry and Henrietta when you come back from the Land of Nod. And then Henry and Henrietta will remember their Adventure as if were yesterday. Normally nobody knows what their Pixie-selves have been up to while they were asleep, beyond the odd strange snippet of dream."

"I see," said Pilgrim Crow. "Thank you."

The Queen sighed and added: "I think our interview is over now. Off you go. I'm going for a little nap."

As Pilgrim was ushered out of Queen Mumbie-Bumbee's front door, he wondered, "How on earth am I going to find the Dodongs?"

CHAPTER THREE.   **Fluff and Nonsense.**

Pilgrim Crow flew directly towards the rocky ridge of Brimstone where he had last met the Dodongs by the Writing-desk rock. It was the only place he could think of.

He landed by the rock and strutted up and down and around, looking for some tell-tale sign of the mighty bird, like a fallen tail feather, perhaps. But tail-feather there was none.

He despondently flew up to the rock and was scanning the horizon when suddenly a shiny mark caught his eye, scrawled on the desk-lid.

"We was here, we was." It read just like a naughty schoolboy might write, thought Pilgrim. Here was another: "Dodongs, so was he."

"Hmm," thought Pilgrim, "it couldn't be the Dodongs who wrote it, because it says, 'Dodongs, so was he,' so who could it be? And do they know where he is now?"

"Hello," a little voice derailed Pilgrim's train of thought. Pilgrim looked about him. He couldn't see anyone. "Where are you?" he asked.

"I'm here, and I'm not coming out till you promise not to eat me," said the squeaky, slightly hollow-sounding voice, a bit like when someone talks into an empty tin can.

"I wouldn't dream of it," replied Pilgrim. "Why would I want to eat you?"

"Birds do," it replied. "Most birds, anyway. But not the Dodongs," it added. "The Dodongs protects us. It's our friend."

"I'm looking for the Dodongs!" cried Pilgrim in delight. "Do you know where he is? Did you write this on the desk-top here?"

"Yes we did, we did," it answered. "That is, we did know, and we did write it. But we don't know now. He dropped us, you know. So we're waiting till he comes back."

"So he's coming back?" cried Pilgrim. "When?"

"Er, we don't know. It was an accident, you see," said the little hidden fellow, "and he might not have missed us yet. But he will."

"Where are you?" called Pilgrim. "I won't eat you, I promise."

"Oh, alright. We're here, under the desk top," it said. "Wait a minute. We'll come out."

Pilgrim waited and waited until eventually a small pair of eyes on the end of little stalks peered over the edge of the rock at him. "Promise?" It asked.

Slowly the eyes were followed by the stripy domed shape of a small small snail. Pilgrim could see now how the scrawly writing had been made. It was the snail's slimy trail he had seen shining on the desk-top.

"We know where he lives," said the snail in its shrill tinny voice, "but we can't get back on our own, you see."

"But how did you get here?" asked Pilgrim.

"On his back, of course," it answered. "We lives there, we do. We cleans his scales, you see."

"Oh, I see," said Pilgrim, "perhaps if you guided me, I could take you there. I could put you safe on my hat-rim and we could fly there."

"What a good idea, but you won't drop us, will you? We're not used to heights."

"Where's the other snail?" asked Pilgrim, "I can only see one of you, but you call yourselves 'We'."

"There's just us," it said, "we just got used to calling ourselves 'We' because we only talk to the Dodongs, and it is a 'We' too, you know."
Pilgrim bent forward and picked up the little snail and carefully placed it on his hat.

"Off we go," he said, as he took off, "hold on tight!"

They flew over the rocky ridge of Brimstone, over the Great Raven Rock, and over the Holywood, until suddenly the snail cried, "there it is! Over there."

Pilgrim saw the gnarled form of an ancient Cedar below him standing on its own in the middle of a park, with rather a grand house facing it.   He flew towards the house.

"Not there, not there!" cried the little snail. "The tree. He lives in the tree."

Pilgrim landed by the tree and strutted towards its base. There, in the fork of a low branch, sat the Dodongs in a clumsily built nest of twigs.

"We're back," cried the little snail, "It's us, Nid-Nod. It's us, Snails."

"Snails, my dears!" cried the Dodongs in glee, "Where have you been? My scales are quite dull with neglect. Where did you get to, you dear things?"

"You dropped us," scolded Snail, "you dropped us by the Writing Desk Rock, and we've been waiting ever since."

"I'm so glad you're back," said the Dodongs, gently picking the snail in one of its beaks and lifting it onto its back. "And you, Sir, how may we repay you for returning our dear, dear friends to us? Tell us, how can we repay you, Sir?"

Pilgrim Crow looked at the Dodongs square in the faces: "I'm Pilgrim Crow. You may remember me. I met you up by that very rock."

They replied, "Of, course. Of course. And how are you this fine morning?"

"I'm very well, thank you for asking," answered Pilgrim, "and you?"

"We're, well..." the Dodongs looked at each other, "...two! But both well too, aren't we?"

Since they both had said this together, the Dodongs realised there was no one to reply to their question, and there was an embarrassed pause.

"Umm, well, of course we are," they both answered at once.

"But the reason I've come is because we've got an emergency," Pilgrim chipped in hastily, "and I need your help."

"An emergency?" repeated the Dodongs, looking thoroughly alarmed. "What sort of emergency? We don't like emergencies, do we?"

"No, we like peace and quiet."

"Emergencies pop up out of nowhere..."

"Like snakes!"

"Like an earthquake!" The Dodongs shuddered as if the ground were about to open up underneath them, and started hopping from foot to foot as getting ready to run off immediately.

"But what's this emergency?" asked the Dodongs. "We'll help if we can."

"Well, it's a long story," began Pilgrim.

"Oh, good. We love stories," said Nid.

"The longer the better," nodded Nod.

"Well," began Pilgrim again, "once upon a time there was a pair of twins..."

"Twins! Did you hear that, Nid?" cried Nod.

"I did, I did!" cried Nid excitedly.

"Just like us!" cried Nod.

"How wonderful!" they both cried, clapping their stubby hands loudly against their sides and nodding furiously.

"Do they look like us?" asked Nod.

"No." replied Pilgrim. "They have two bodies, not two heads on one body."

"How silly."

"How ridiculous."

"That's not proper twins. Proper twins have two heads, like us…"

"So they can tell each other's thoughts."

"But they can," cried Pilgrim, "They can tell each other's thoughts. So they are like you, sort of. They were born together at the same time."

"Hatched, you mean," said Nid.

"A double yolker, probably," said Nod.

"We almost like them already, don't we, Nod?" said Nid.

"We do, we do, Nid," said Nod, "do continue."

"Well," began Pilgrim Crow for the third time. "Once upon a time there was a pair of twins, Henry and Henrietta…"

"How awful," cried Nid. His large head nodded in distress. He breathed in, sighed out loudly.

"How tragic!" cried Nod in sympathy, as his large head too nodded up, sighed down.

Seizing his chance Pilgrim Crow dashed forward and snatched the Magic Down (Down is the softest fluffy feathers a bird has) the Dodongs had sighed out before they noticed what had happened, and hid it under his hat.

"How tragic," cried the Dodongs, "why did Henry eat her?"

"No, no. Henry didn't eat anyone," started Pilgrim.

"Oh, thank goodness for that," the Dodongs heaved another, smaller sigh of relief.

"We're vegetarians, you know," nodded Nid (the left hand head; if you can have a left hand-head, that is).

"We think eating your friends is frightfully greedy," added Nod.

"We don't agree with greediness, do we?"

"It's so bad for the digestion," said Nod.

"But it wasn't much of a story then, was it, if they didn't eat each other," said Nid, a little huffily.

"Not much at all," said Nod, nodding.

"That's not the story," said Pilgrim testily, "I haven't even begun it yet."

"So what's the story about then?" they asked.

"Henry and Henrietta," replied an exasperated Pilgrim.

"Then you have begun it," said Nid.

"You just haven't finished it," said Nod.

"Henry and Henrietta…" began Pilgrim.

"When can we meet them?" interrupted Nid.

"Yes, when are they coming?" said Nod.

"We're dying to meet them," said the Dodongs both together.

"Well, that's the problem," said Pilgrim, "they are both dying, we think. That's why I'm here."

"Dying, you say?" cried the Dodongs in alarm (they were easily alarmed).

"How tragic," cried Nid as his deep breathing in sighed out.

"Yes, how tragically sad," cried Nod, as his large head nodded up, sighed down.

Seizing his chance Pilgrim Crow dashed forward and snatched the Magic Down the Dodongs had just sighed out before they noticed what had happened, and hid it under his hat.

(You might think I have said that already. But this was a second Magic Downy feather. He had to get two Feathers, one for each of the twins.)

Having got his two Downy Feathers without getting caught, Pilgrim Crow bowed deeply and said: "I'm afraid something's come up and I've got to go straightaway. Goodbye!"

With that, he launched himself into the air without further "Adieu" and flew off as fast as his little wings could carry him.

"Well, fancy that!" cried Nid, "how rude!"

"What got into him?" cried Nod, "and I thought he was such a nice boy."

"He never told us about Henry and Henrietta, neither," added Nod.

"Nor he did," nodded Nid.

"Nor us, neither, he didn't," added Snail, significantly.

Pilgrim crow flew as fast as he could back from the Great Cypress where the Dodongs perched to Writing Desk Rock, so that he could get his bearings to find his way Home, where the Twins lived.

From the top of the desk he flew down to the Old Hawthorn where Queen Mumbie lived, and so on until he found his way Home.

And if you want to see how the Animals hid the Magic Down under Henry and Henrietta's pillows and how Pixie-Henry and Pixie-Henrietta emerged from their cocoons like butterflies and how they all went off to the Great Land of Nod to meet the Dodongs, the Ineffable Emperor of the great Sea of Slumber, which is all around us, if only see could see it, and of all the creatures they met there and the Great Adventure that was there, just waiting to be had. Well, then …